Mrs Pinto Drives to Happiness
and Other Stories

Reshma Ruia

First published 2021 by Dahlia Publishing Ltd
ISBN 9781913624057

Copyright © Reshma Ruia 2021

The moral right of the author has been asserted.

Some of the stories in this collection have appeared elsewhere, in a slightly different form:

Cookery Lessons in Suburbia in *In the Kitchen* (Dahlia Books), Cooking Chicken in Kentucky in *No Good Deed*, A Simple Man in *May We Borrow Your Country* (Linen Press), A Birthday Gift in *Leicester Writes Short Story Prize 2018* (Dahlia Books), Mrs Pinto Drives to Happiness in *The Nottingham Review*, Soul Sisters in *Love Across A Broken Map* (Dahlia Books), The Lodger in *The Mechanics' Institute Review*.

Printed and bound by Grosvenor Group

A CIP catalogue record for this book is available from The British Library.

'I suppose in the end, the whole of life becomes an act of letting go'
— Yann Martel, Life of Pi

For Raj, Ravi, Sabrina
The compass to my world

CONTENTS

Mrs Pinto Drives to Happiness

Every Friday Mrs Pinto receives her wages inside a cream envelope. Her employer, Mrs Ibrahim may lock the pantry door at night but there are certain courtesies she insists on observing. She hands Mrs Pinto the envelope with a slight bow. 'For you, Mrs Pinto,' she says and turns to her mobile phone ready to plot luncheon and shopping excursions with her friends.

Mrs Pinto thanks her, her right hand pressed to her chest to show her appreciation.

'Before you go, make sure to mop the bathroom floor.' Mrs Ibrahim's voice is distracted.

'Yes Madam,' Mrs Pinto says. They both know she has cleaned the entire house from attic to cellar that very morning.

The bathroom is bigger than Mrs Pinto's entire house in Canacona. She can eat choris pão off the floor if she wanted, but she still kneels down, her fingers running like a searchlight on the marble tiles. Not a speck of dirt. Mrs Pinto straightens herself and pauses in front of the mirror. There, she stood. All six foot of her. 'Gangly like a coconut tree. Who is going to marry you?' her mother had wailed. Mrs Pinto unties her white apron and quietly runs a hand over her waist - still svelte despite the years of scrubbing and cleaning. There is life in her yet, she thinks as she walks to the shelf where the golden perfume bottles stand rigid like

1

soldiers in a firing squad. She twists open a lid and sniffs the perfume. This isn't her world. Mrs Pinto accepts that. She may be a graduate in public administration from St. Maria's College of Higher Education, but at the age of forty she's taking orders from a chit of a girl with big bouncy hair who hasn't done a day's work in her life. But what's the point in grumbling. She knows her week's salary here is worth a month's back home.

In her attic room, Mrs Pinto, eyes narrowed, carefully counts her money before storing it inside a white shoebox. It will stay there until Tuesday afternoon, when she catches the 230 bus from the corner of Park Lane near the Hilton hotel to Edgeware Road.

'Let me drop you, habibi,' Ahmed the driver says. He is outside, flicking a yellow dust cloth over the bonnet of the blue Mercedes. She shakes her head. It's not the first time he has called her beloved.

'Thank you, but I prefer to take the bus.' She likes to climb up to the top and sit at the front, the sprawl of the city beneath her, her box nestled between her thighs.

He shrugs. 'I'll walk you to the bus stop.' They walk in silence with Ahmed whistling. She recognises the tune.

'How come you sing when you see me?' she asks. Ahmed has curly hair and a husky voice. At night when she has trouble sleeping, she squeezes her eyes shut and imagines him riding camels across sand dunes, his white robes like a splash of milk.

He laughs. 'I only sing when I see your swaying hips

2

habibi. You are my Bollywood heroine.'

Mrs Pinto's mouth trembles into a smile but she lifts a finger in warning. 'I'm a married woman, so don't you be trying any hanky-panky with me.'

'A joke, habibi. You know I'm a true gentleman.' He winks.

The mobile in Ahmed's pocket vibrates. 'Ach... Madam want me.' He slaps the side of his head in mock despair and imitates her high-pitched voice, 'Ali take me here. Drop me there. Allah gave her two good legs. She needs to use them, not save them for a rainy day.'

Mrs Pinto purses her lips and pretends to look severe. 'Don't forget she pays our salary.'

'One day, I'll take you to see the bright lights of Blackpool. We'll drive there in the Mercedes.' Ahmed's eyes shine as he turns to her. 'Promise me, habibi?'

'Maybe,' she says. She knows Ahmed's English life started in Blackpool. It was where he got his residency papers while working in a fish and chip shop. Blackpool is the most beautiful city in the world for him. 'The lights at night are like a necklace of diamonds and the cold air is good for your soul.' She had googled Blackpool once and was shocked to see pictures of boarded up shops and sea the colour of dishwater. Still she humours him, 'Yes. We will go to Blackpool one day.'

Mrs Pinto gets off at the Western Union shop. She feels important as she signs her name and counts the money twice before nudging it through the hole in the glass partition. Mrs Pinto likes her excursion to Edgeware Road. The summer sky above her is pasty yellow like moong dal. Her coat, one of Mrs Ibrahim's hand me downs, feels snug and warm around her broad shoulders. She wanders among the shops. Their gutter glitter spilling on the pavements remind her of Canacona and her son and husband weaving their way across such a street, elbowing their way through the crowds to reach her.

'When are you coming home, Ma?' her son asks her in their weekly Skype conversations. He throws her the question like a cricket ball and then runs outside to play. He's happy even if he misses her. Matthew, her husband is her bigger worry. Where was that smiling man with the handlebar moustache who had taken her to eat garlic crabs on the Palolem beach? The man who stood mumbling across the screen has sunken cheeks and hooded eyes that hide secrets.

He talks of money, always money, not of how she passes her days so far from home. 'We need money. Mary. Do what you have to do.' His face dissolves inside the blue mercury buzz of the laptop screen before swimming back in focus. The words fade and his eyes do a dance, one moment he's staring at the floor, next looking at something behind her shoulder. Rarely do his eyes return to her waiting face.

'The roof is leaking and Raju needs a new school uniform. I have to buy new painkillers.' His life is one long shopping list and it is her job to tick off each item. She listens patiently. Poor Matthew, what can he do? An accident in the garment factory where he worked had turned his left arm into mince. He was now only good for grumbling and gambling.

Mrs Pinto's steps falter as she thinks of her husband. She must try to be a good wife and earn more. She makes the sign of a cross and whispers Amen. She still has sturdy limbs and a head that never loses its cool. She is proud to be the breadwinner, working twelve hours a day so her family has air-conditioning and new clothes to wear to the Christmas Mass. She will simply ask Mrs Ibrahim for a loan.

∞

'It's to repair the roof,' she says.

'What roof are you talking about? Our house is good.'

Their eyes meet in the mirror. Mrs Pinto sighs. She needs to simplify and elaborate her request to the woman who sits hunched in front of the dressing table painting her eyebrows with a crayon.

Mrs Pinto begins again.

'I need extra money to repair the roof of my house in Canacona. The monsoons are coming. My son also needs a new school uniform.' She pauses. Mrs Ibrahim's hands have wandered to her mouth, which she is painting grape red.

'School uniforms are expensive in Canacona.' Mrs Pinto finishes.

Mrs Ibrahim swivels around on her pink fur-lined chair. She scratches her chin.

'I didn't know you had a son.'

Mrs Pinto draws herself to her full height. 'He is thirteen. I left him when he was ten, and my husband is...' She searches for the right word, 'Mutilated, incapacitated, handicapped, failure, drunkard, womaniser.' 'He is disabled because of an accident at work. He has lost an arm.'

Mrs Ibrahim's eyebrows rise. 'That must have hurt,' she says.

'That is why I came to England to work. I left my son behind.'

She remembers the day and her early flight. She had left her son fast asleep, the bedsheet tangled around his little legs, his mouth open in a half-smile.

'Okay I will ask my husband. He will decide.'

That night Mrs Pinto turns on the laptop and her husband's face floats into view. There is an ugly twist to his mouth as his words tumble out. 'Bitch. Whore. Send me more money. Fast.'

∞

She's in the kitchen preparing dinner. Chopped onions sit in a pile on the chopping board. They are the reason for her red-rimmed eyes.

'Mrs Pinto.'

Mr Ibrahim stands at the door. He's wearing loose jogging bottoms with gold entwined Gs splashed all over it.

'Good afternoon, Sir.' She bows her head and waits. Maybe he is after a snack. Some falafel.

'Do you want a raise?' he asks, one foot swinging as he

leans against the doorframe.

'I want a loan. I will pay it back,' Mrs Pinto replies. Her eyes itch and she rubs at it with the hem of her sleeve.

He comes closer and she smells his tobacco breath.

His hand shoots out and cups her breast. 'How are you going to pay me back?' He says as he kneads her breast. She pushes him away and runs to her room.

Mr Ibrahim is normally a benign shadow that occupies the rooms and leaves behind traces of his existence but is never actually there.

'He spends a lot of time in the Gulf,' Mrs Ibrahim had confided in her at the start of her employment.

'Very important business.' And Mrs Pinto had nodded, humbled at the chance of working in such an illustrious man's house.

∞

It's only at night when the moon is high and the roar of traffic dimmed to a purr that Mrs Pinto allows the trembling in her bones to ease. She peers at herself in the small round mirror that hangs above the sink. She must see her face. Ahmed had told her, the face is the gatekeeper to the soul. There's her mouth with its downward droop and her eyes wide and slanting, the colour of brown toast. She strokes her cheek, her fingers light like feather.

The shrill squeak of her mobile wakes her. It is 6 am but almost lunchtime in Canacona. Her son's tearful voice says that the father has gone missing. 'He left holding a bottle of whiskey in his good hand,' the boy whimpers. She tells him to go to his grandmother's house.

Mrs Pinto is tired of holding up her world.

∞

She wakes up late next morning.

Mrs Ibrahim taps her gold watch. 'I had to give breakfast to my children all on my own and the kitchen is a mess and I'm late for my hairdresser.' Her bottom lip juts out and she scowls.

There is a strange fire burning in Mrs Pinto's eyes as she stares at her employer. She says she will start cleaning the bedrooms. Methodically, concentrating hard, she whips off the bedsheets from the beds and throws them on the floor. She enters the bathroom and gathers the lotions, pouring the contents into the toilet. She empties the vases of their flowers and leaves them strewn on the carpet. She finds Mr Ibrahim's tracksuit bottoms and scissors through it until it is like shredded confetti.

She goes outside. A purple balloon floats high above. The cherry trees shiver with flower and Ahmed is whistling as he polishes the hubcaps of the Mercedes. He straightens up when he sees her and raises his an eyebrow.

Mrs Pinto smiles. 'Where's Madam?'

'At the hairdressers. She's not happy with you. Says you're a lazy good for nothing.' He shakes his head.

Mrs Pinto considers this as she stands, her face raised to the sky to catch the sun's warmth. She stretches out her hands and examines her palms. There runs her lifeline, long and strong. She won't let anyone halt its flow.

Opening the car door, she slips into the passenger seat and pats the empty driver's seat beside her.

'Come on Ahmed. What are we waiting for? It's a wonderful day. We're driving to Blackpool to see the lights.'

First Love and other Betrayals

A grey haired woman wearing round steel framed glasses is waiting for him in the arrivals hall. She holds up a piece of paper with his name scrawled in red felt tip.

He points to the name.

'Neel. That's me.'

'Hello Neel. I'm Bemke. Do you remember me? I'm Mugenzi's sister?' Her voice rises at the end so that the statement comes across as a question.

He attempts to hug her, but it's an awkward sideways embrace as he's still holding on to his suitcase.

'It's been a long time, isn't that so?' Bemke says stepping out of his arms.

'You are still very much the same,' he lies. He would have passed her on the street without recognising her. His grip tightens on his suitcase handle.

She steps back, hand on her chin, surveying him. 'And you Mister Neel are very much changed. How did you get to be so well fed? Life must be good in England.'

They laugh and then stop, as though remembering the reason for their meeting.

'I'm glad you managed to track me down.' Neel lowers his voice.

She shrugs. 'All thanks to Sir Google. The world is a small place when there is sad news to share. No one can hide anymore.'

The e-mail was brief. It said that Mugenzi was dead. He had been ill for some time. It did not mention the disease, but Neel had guessed. The funeral would be held at St. Michaels Baptist church in Kigali. In lieu of flowers, donations were directed to Kigali Hospital's department of autoimmune disease.

'I could have taken a taxi to the hotel. You shouldn't have taken the trouble.' His English spills out foreign and pompous.

Bemke imitates Neel's formal tone. 'It was no bother at all. You are Mugenzi's oldest friend. It's the least I can do for a dead man.'

They step outside into the shimmer of the mid-day sun. Neel reaches for his sunglasses. The airport has expanded since he last saw it. In place of the prefabricated shed stands a steel and glass building. A large billboard leans against a wall. It shows a young white couple snuggling on a beach, sipping Coca Cola. 'We guarantee happiness,' the red tagline screams. Men in high-vis jackets scuttle around, holding ropes and ladders, trying to hoist the billboard up onto the airport roof. Dewdrops of sweat sparkle on their foreheads.

The familiar sound of crickets chirping and the cawing of the Hadada Ibis rises from the trees across the barbed wire boundary fence. The heat floats up like mist from the asphalt car park, catches Neel's throat, turning it dry.

There are neat parking bays demarcated in white. A large blue and white board advises the motorists that parking charges for all vehicles are 3000 RWF for the first hour.

'Wow! This is all very new and glossy,' Neel says. 'When did Rwanda change?'

Bemke smiles. 'All courtesy of Chinese money. The British left and the Chinese stepped in after the killings.' She wrinkles her nose. 'What is that proverb you British say… nature abhors a vacuum.'

Neel spots the sky blue Opel Kadett with the z-shaped dent on its side. 'Oh my God, you've still got the same car!'

'You remember it?' Bemke raises an eyebrow.

'Ugly Helga'. They'd christened the car, her brother and him. When night fell, Mugenzi would sneak to his house; throw stones at his bedroom window until Neel looked out. There he stood, Mugenzi in his white vest and tight blue jeans, beckoning him down. Neel had tiptoed out; shoes held against his chest, frightened that his parents would wake up and catch him sneaking out in the thick of night. Then the long drive in Ugly Helga to Lake Muhazi. Parking in the shadows of the Acacia tree, under a dark-peppered sky, windows wound down to let in the cool blue of the night. The smell of the leather seats, the slow yet hurried unbuttoning and unzipping. Skin brushing against skin and the shared cigarette afterwards with Ella Fitzgerald moaning on the radio about a 'paper moon.' How could Neel forget it?

He glances at the back seat now as Bemke opens the car door.

'Why didn't you buy another car? A Japanese one with automatic gears?'

Bemke grins and announces in a singsong voice as though reading an advertising jingle, 'German cars. By your side for your next seven lives. Wasn't that your father's line? See, I've not forgotten.'

Neel's father owned the only car dealership in Kigali. Standing proud among his cars, he would announce that only German cars were fit for African roads. 'They have Teutonic tyres,' he told prospective customers. He had sold Bemke her first and only car.

Bemke takes Neel's suitcase and swings it inside the boot.

'It's light as a cloud. Aren't you going to take a tour of the mother country? Visit your old haunts?'

He shakes his head. 'I have work to get back to. Maybe next time.'

They make polite talk on the way to the hotel.

'How was the flight?' Bemke asks her eyes fixed on the road crowded with motorcyclists and women walking with baskets of yam and plantains on their heads. A small child runs onto the road chasing a blue striped beach ball. She swears and swerves. Neel lurches forward, his head inches from the windscreen.

'Sorry, the life belt's broken,' Bemke says.

'You mean seat belt,' Neel says laughing, placing a reassuring hand on her thigh. 'Don't worry, I'm still here.'

But Mugenzi is not. His death rides in the car with them like a third passenger, accompanying them all the way to the Kigali Serena where Neel has booked a two-night stay.

'How did he die? Was he very ill?' he asks Bemke when

13

they are almost at the hotel.

She moistens her lips and stares ahead.

'It was not AIDS. He was not fashionable enough for that. He caught a drink problem, mixing the wrong kind of liquor and men.' Bemke's laugh is a dry bone rattle. 'You could have saved him from himself. You know that, don't you?'

'I told him to apply for government funding and come to England. He didn't want to try. I moved house and lost his address and then it became too late.' The words stick in Neel's throat.

Bemke shakes her head.

'It's always too late, isn't it? Mugenzi didn't have survival skills like you…he was always…eh…angry as a rhino and slow as a snail. Anyway, we got him married. My parents thought it would be good, a woman in his life to tie down his wandering feet.' She lifts a hand and then places it back on the steering wheel.

At the hotel gates, the guard stops the car, opens the boot and runs a metal rod over the contents to check for explosives. He waves them through after noting down the car registration number in a brown notebook.

'Are there many coming to the funeral?' Neel is back to making small talk.

Bemke nods. 'Yes, there are cousins coming from as far as Jo 'burg. Mugenzi was well liked.' Her bottom lip sags as she says this and she takes off her glasses and wipes them on her sleeve.

The hotel lobby is designed to resemble a local hut. Tall Aloe Vera plants stand stiff in woven coir baskets and brass hurricane lamps swing from the ceiling. A khaki uniformed UN Peacekeeper sits on a sofa, mobile phone pushed close to his ear.

The receptionist lifts her head from the computer screen and smiles at them expectantly.

'You're sure you'll be alright here?' Bemke asks Neel again.

'I'm a big boy.' He chuckles.

'It's just that you've been away so long. Your bones must have gone clay soft in the London rain,' she says, translating an old Tutsi saying.

'I was born here,' he reminds her.

Still she hesitates, her right index finger tapping the side of her cheek. She gives a sudden shudder, pulls herself straight and looks at her watch.

'Be careful, Neel. Lock your door. Don't go out in the dark. It's a five-star hotel, but it is still Rwanda, right. Death is always waiting around the corner.' Finger wagging in warning, she walks away.

∞

The hotel gets busier as the night deepens. Neel goes down to the bar. A single bottle of Johnny Walker along with three bottles of Virunga beer perch on a yellow Perspex shelf next to a signed framed photo of the President.

The receptionist is doubling up as a bartender. She has

15

swapped her striped jacket for a red halter neck. An indigo tattoo of a butterfly flutters on her collarbone.

'Are you with the World Bank?' she asks, pouring Neel a whiskey.

'I am here for a friend's funeral,' he explains in a way that stops further questioning. She murmurs a so sorry and turns to attend to a group of Chinese businessmen sitting precariously on bar stools, their briefcases snug in their lap, their feet not quite touching the faded jute carpet with its swirl of yellow flowers.

The lobby is busy with UN types wearing navy blazers and clutching bright coloured folders. Neel glances at his own jacket. He could be one of them. It was his mother's dearest wish.

'Don't end up selling second-hand cars like your father,' she said on his school graduation day, her mouth slack with disappointment.

'You've got a brain. Get a job in a big multinational. In the UN. Get out of Africa.'

Neel did that. Gained a scholarship to a British university where he quickly excelled and made friends with a string of well-connected boys whose fathers offered him internships.

Mugenzi came to see him the day he was leaving for England. Neel was in his bedroom, packing, emptying his room of the detritus of his youth. Mugenzi shut the door behind him.

'Is this how you leave me, Neel? You think it's so easy to get away.' He spat on the floor and pulled a penknife from his pocket. Grabbing Neel's wrist, he made a small cut. The blood trickled out in small hesitant drops and then Mugenzi cut his own wrist. 'This is how it should be,' Mugenzi whispered as he pressed their two wounded wrists together, the blood mingling, becoming one. His arm snaked around Neel's waist, and his fingers slid down, pressing against his hipbone. 'We belong together. Never forget that,' Mugenzi said.

Afterwards Mugenzi lingered by the door but Neel's mother didn't invite him to stay for dinner. She didn't approve of Neel's friendship with a local boy.

'I don't know what you see in that waste -of –time. Stick to your own kind,' she said.

∞

He dreams of Mugenzi that night. Mugenzi with his arrow-straight black back and his slanting, grass green eyes, the result of a freak genetic accident sits on the edge of his bed. 'You forgot me too quickly, Neel. Why?' The body arches forward towards him, tearing away his clothes, folding him in an embrace inside his broad, impatient arms, drawing him in deep until Neel can take no more.

'Forgive me, Mugenzi. Forgive me for leaving you behind,' Neel screams and wakes up.

The hotel has had a power failure through the night and the air is damp and heavy. Neel lies still, the bedspread clinging to him in a glue of sweat, watching a procession of cockroaches sidle out from beneath the wardrobe and make their way across the floor to the skirting board. It is early but he can sense the thick spill of the daylight heat waiting behind the drawn curtains.

His mobile shrills into life. It's his wife. He tells her the flight was fine and he's safe.

'I should have come with you. I've always wanted to see Africa,' she says. Her voice turns sulky and peevish.

'There's nothing to see here. I will be busy in meetings and the kids. You can't leave them on their own.'

It had been simpler to say to his wife that he was going to Rwanda on work.

He gets up, walks to the window and flings it open, lifting his face to the sky where the sun floats like an orange helium balloon.

∞

The wide expanse of Livingstone road, Kigali's first modern road built with an IMF loan ends abruptly, tapers into a muddy red footpath about two hundred yards from St. Michaels Church. Flanking it on one side is the jackfruit tree of Neel's childhood. The chalk painted white walls of the church stand sharply etched against the russet silhouette of the Albertine Rift Mountains. Neel shuts his eyes. There they are – Mugenzi and him, running to the church and hiding behind the jackfruit tree, squatting in the dust, playing marbles, forgetting the moon, the stars, the sun. It would be nightfall before Bemke came hollering at Mugenzi. Her shrill voice slicing the thin silence of the night.

'Mugenzi... it is time to come home. Mugenzi...'

A small group stands at the foot of the steps, the women in red and green mushanana robes, the men wearing dark coloured jackets and ill-fitting trousers over sandaled feet. They turn around and stare as Neel takes his place among them. He does not recognise them. A hand touches his arm. It is an old woman, dressed in yellow, a blue checked turban wrapped around her head.

'You're Salim's son. Can it be so? Neel? You are Neel?'

He nods.

'You remember my father? Mister Salim?' His family did not stick around for long after his own departure for England. They smelled the whiff of trouble blowing in and packing their bags in a hurry left the country in the stealth of night just as the civil war broke out. Their house was looted and the garage with its fleet of ten German cars torched soon after.

'They were going to kill us,' his mother had cried over the telephone line from Toronto.

'To think how much your father has done for that country. Gave them jobs, sold them cars on credit and this is the gratitude we get. Thank God your aunt Salma in Canada was able to sponsor us and we could make a fresh start.' His mother died a few years later, a disappointed woman reduced to stacking shelves in a 7-Eleven in Toronto, secretly hankering after the African sun of her youth.

The old woman jabs Neel's arm again.

19

'Mr Salim was a good man, but he ran away like a thief.'

It comes back to him. She is Mrs Tsonga, the widow who'd helped his father with the accounts. She was a graduate and spoke English and his father had employed her. They worked late in the garage, hunched over the notebooks, the single dangling light bulb, throwing a halo of light over their bent heads, glancing up only when Neel appeared with a tiffin full of rice and fried okra for their dinner.

'My father tried his best to be a good man,' Neel says.

His father discovered his secret by chance. It was Neel's final year at university and he had stayed behind on the campus for the winter break. He was dating someone then, a blond, blue-eyed boy whose name he can't remember anymore. His father, paying a surprise visit had walked in on them while they were in bed, arms entwined around each other. So many years but Neel still remembered the knock on the door and the silence that followed.

His father had died like his mother, holding the wedge of bitterness tight within the folds of his heart.

'The shame of it,' he muttered as he lay dying on the hospital bed. 'Promise me you will mend your ways. Neel, promise me you will marry a girl and settle down.'

'I promise,' Neel said, holding on to his father's arm, watching the light dim in his eyes. The pain of disappointing his father squeezed his chest until he felt lightheaded. The following year he married a family friend's daughter. It was his way of atoning.

There is a shuffle, a gasp and the crowd parts to make way for the funeral cortege. The timber coffin, borne high by four young men in tight black suits passes like a ship sailing above the heads of the mourners.

'They are Mugenzi's brother in laws. Fine young men all of them,' Mrs Tsonga whispers. She fans herself with a Chinese fan painted with red dragons.

'Mugenzi was happily married?' Neel wants to be sure.

'Mugenzi was happily married,' Bemke says. She has stepped out of the crowd of mourners to find him. She clasps his hand.

'You must pay respects to your friend.' She nudges Neel forward until he stands in front of the altar.

The pews are taken but she finds a space for him on the front row. He sits near a woman whose face is hidden behind a black gauze veil. She keeps wringing her hands. Pressed between her fingers is a ball of damp tissue. The four boys who had carried the coffin sit on her left. Their long dangly knees protrude from neatly pressed black trousers. They hunch forward to hear better the priest who is welcoming his congregation.

Neel doesn't hear Reverent Daniel's words. He looks at the coffin resting on the stone slab. A photograph of a younger smiling Mugenzi sits on top of the coffin. It stares back at him. In the photograph, Mugenzi wears a Yankees baseball cap roguishly tilted over his eyes. Neel recognises the cap. It was an eighteenth birthday present from him.

'That's just what I wanted,' Mugenzi had said, grabbing

the cap, turning it inside and out, reading the label.

'It's the real stuff. How did you get it, Neel?'

'My aunt in Canada. I begged her to send me one.' Neel had shrugged, making light of the present. 'It's no big deal,' he said, but deep within, his heart had somersaulted with joy, watching Mugenzi fling the cap in the air and catch it, before pulling it low over his head. 'Don't I look good, Neel, eh, your own Michael Jackson.'

The service finishes and the church empties but Neel lingers behind. Reverent Daniel, his long white robes floating in the gloomy darkness approaches him, grasping his hands.

'Is that you, Neel? Welcome home.'

'I should have come sooner,' Neel mumbles. He slips his hands in his pockets. They are soggy with sweat.

'You should not have forgotten your own,' the priest replies. 'Mugenzi's answered God's call. He was never the same after you were gone. He looked up to you like a brother.'

'I invited him to England.' Neel swallows and continues. 'Mugenzi dropped out of school. He should have stuck at it. Tried for a scholarship, like I did.'

Except Neel knows better. He knows that he never invited Mugenzi, never sent him an air ticket or even a postcard. What could a poor village boy who barely spoke English do in his bright new world?

Reverent Daniel bows his head, his eyes on the coffin. There will be only a quiet cremation away from the crowds.

'It was Mugenzi's wishes.' The priest had explained at the end of the service. 'Mugenzi wants to die alone. He don't want nobody's judging eyes.'

∞

Neel enters Mugenzi's house by the back door. Mrs Tsonga and a gaggle of older women hover over the stove, taking turns to stir the pot. There is a smell of matoke frying and boiling meat.

'Goat curry,' Mrs Tsonga explains, catching his eye. 'It was Mugenzi's favourite dish.'

But Neel knows that already. On the last Saturday of the month, Mugenzi and he caught the interstate bus to the main square in Nyabugogo where vendors displayed their wares on blue and white checked Tenke cloth. The air was heavy with the smell of cow dung and rotting ripe plantains. Holding hands, they jostled against each other, fingertips electric with desire, their love a secret, safe among the thick throng of people. Hamza's stall was at the farthest end of the market, next to Tambo who sold birds to wealthy landowners to keep as pets. The squawking quails and parrots with plumage dyed in rainbow colours fretfully paced their cages and Mugenzi, with a wink and a quick sleight of hand, would snap open the cage doors, setting the birds free. Puffed up with the sense of their daring, they'd whistle and walk on before turning back to make their way to Hamza's stall.

'Hamza's goat curry is the best, man. But always ask for

23

the neck,' Mugenzi proclaimed each time, smacking his lips. They ate the curry mixed up with rice and green chillies as fat as fingers, squatting on the red earth, grinning with happiness while the world spun around them.

∞

The women push Neel towards the front room where Mugenzi's family is waiting to receive the mourners. Heads lowered, they listen as the guests breathe words of condolence and take a sip from the large earthen pot of sorghum beer that stands in the centre of the room.

Neel dips a steel tumbler into the pot and finishes the beer in one swig. His stomach growls from lack of food. He feels the thrum of a headache behind his eyelids.

'Go, meet Victoria. Comfort the dead man's wife,' the women shout again.

Victoria sits on a low stool, her hands on her stomach. The veil has gone, as has the black dress. She has changed into a grey pinafore. A blue straw hat rests like a bird on her head.

Neel crouches down so his face is level with hers.

'I am sorry for your loss, Victoria.' He feels foolish saying her name. Its primness doesn't match the wide open fullness of her face.

Her dark eyes gleam with sorrow.

She frowns, breaths in deeply and takes a sip of water from the tumbler on the floor. Leaning forward she clasps Neel's hand between hers, pressing his fingers until his knuckles turn pale.

'Thank you. Mugenzi was my world. My first love.'

Teardrops hang from her lower lashes.

Neel bows his head, balls his hand into a fist and beats it gently against his chest.

'He was a good friend of mine,' he says in a low voice.

Rubbing her eyes with the heel of her palm, she looks at him closely.

Her eyes narrow. Her mouth trembles.

Neel stares back, silent. Trapped in her gaze. He can smell the beer on his breath.

'Excuse me, but who are you exactly? I never saw you with him.' Victoria's voice rises.

He is about to introduce himself when there is a commotion at the door. Reverent Daniel arrives bearing Mugenzi's ashes in a plastic supermarket bag. The women begin ululating and crossing themselves.

'Don't leave,' Victoria says to Neel as he gets up to join them. 'I want you to meet someone. Come follow me.'

She walks out of the front door and stands on the porch. A swarm of boys are playing in the dusty patch in front of the house, bare feet kicking a red and white football.

'Goal!' they scream as the ball arcs and disappears over the fence.

'Come here, son,' Victoria shouts. A boy with slanting grass green eyes and the Yankee baseball cap on his head walks slowly up to them.

'Good shot,' Neel says.

25

'Thank you,' the boy answers with a slight lisp.

Victoria reaches out and squeezes his shoulder.

'Your son looks just like Mugenzi. What is his name?'

'He is the dead man's son. The dead man's son.' The other boys set up a chant, clapping their hands and jumping up and down. 'Dead man's son,' they sing in a chorus.

Victoria pulls her son closer. 'His father named him.'

'My name is Neel,' says the boy. 'What's yours?'

The Lodger

Old age. It still catches them by surprise.

'Not that we are terribly old,' Mandy tells the bathroom mirror as she brushes her teeth. She stares at her face as though it was a map that needed a compass.

'How did this happen?' asks Bill, her husband, a protective hand on his heart. He scowls at the rainbow of pills on his plate.

'It's high time you guys moved into a care home. This house is too big and you're too old,' their daughter Abigail observes, lying on the couch. Her left leg is raised as she paints her toenails crimson.

Abigail lives in Nevada on a cactus plantation with a woman who is her girlfriend. They run a hemp oil business. The oil extracted and shipped in neat little silver cartons has the tag line *Grease Up Your Insides*. The Grahams only know this from the company website.

'You sure messed up. Look at the both of you. Not even eighty yet but hobbling around like a pair of whackos. I mean, deal with it,' Abigail says. She uncurls herself and sits up straight, her legs extended, blowing on her newly painted toes one by one. Her quick, healthy puffs of breath dazzle her parents.

'I'm not moving out, if that's what you mean. I'm staying right here,' Mandy says, trying to keep the quiver out of her voice. 'You could visit more often.'

'We could get a lodger,' Bill suggests. His voice dips, small and uncertain. 'He can keep an eye on us and we'd get some income too. It'll be a win win.'

Now that Bill has retired from his job as the maintenance man at Delaunay High School in Chantilly, and Mandy's left knee flares with arthritis every winter, they find their pension isn't enough to cover the expenses of old age.

Bill darts an anxious glance at his daughter. The plan needs her blessing.

Abigail approves. 'Yeah... I like that. A lodger. Some nice guy who keeps an eye on you like you say. He could even help Mom clean up this shit.' Her eyes sweep over the room.

It is late afternoon. The smells of the previous night linger stale in the living room, like a set of unwashed teeth in the morning. Mugs of coffee and Pyrex bowls of microwave-fresh popcorn and cheesy nachos balance on old copies of *Sports Illustrated* and crochet magazines. Mandy sucks Sprite through a straw while listening to her daughter. Her husband dunks his hand in and out of the bowl. From time to time, he sniffs his fingers, inhaling the popcorn's greasy salty smell.

Abigail raises her voice. 'Just look at this mess, Mom.'

Mandy gets up to shut her bedroom door. She doesn't want Abigail to see her unmade bed or the dropped towels that carry red and brown streaks of her make-up like battle wounds.

'Dad's right, Abigail. We'll get someone. The money wouldn't hurt, especially now that Dad's got his angina to deal with.' Mandy pauses, and examines her hands that sit like a pair of discarded gloves on her lap.

A lodger will perk them up; give them an excuse to get out of bed, plump up the cushions, buy the lettuce, change into jeans rather than stay Velcro-strapped inside their elasticated sweatpants.

Mandy continues, 'Did you know that in England you can get your medicines free? That's what the radio said.'

'That's bullshit. Nothing's ever free.' Abigail gives a snort.

'I'll put an ad on Craigslist for the lodger. Dad, get me my iPad will you?'

Bill shuffles out of the room and hands it to her like a trophy. 'There you go, honey.'

Abigail runs her tongue over her bottom lip and pulls at a strand of her dark-brown hair as she hunches over her iPad. Bill eats the popcorn quietly while Mandy trains her eyes on the patched spot on the blue Navajo rug. They had a pet once, a German shepherd who'd chewed his way through the house and had to be put down.

Abigail writes: Elderly retired couple living in a quiet neighbourhood would welcome a lodger. Low rent in exchange for light household help. A well-furnished basement bedroom. Wi-Fi, utilities, and use of kitchen included in the deal. No probing into the past or future. Just be present...

She grins as she reads this out to her parents.

Mandy objects to the ending.

'But, you don't mention the rental amount and what if he

29

is a rapist or a child-molester,' Mandy says.

'Of course, we'll probe. We're Americans not Buddhists.'
Abigail rolls her eyes at her mother's naiveté.

She won't say it, but Mandy is glad about the advert. A
lodger means company. As much as the radio babbles, the
TV gurgles, the husband snores, she can't deny she is lonely.
Not lonely in a vein-cutting, circus-clown way, but alone in
a silent, window-watching way. She spends hours sitting on
her plastic chair on the back step looking at her yard, making
a mental inventory of things each season left behind. In the
summer, there was the barbecue set, burger fat congealed
on its insides, and the paddling pool where tadpoles' breast
stroked in rainwater. Fall came with its shower of fallen
leaves shored up at the borders and the empty hammock
swinging under the bald-headed tree that could be elm or
chestnut, she's never quite sure.

'It'll be good to have company,' she tells her husband
after Abigail has left.

'He can clear the crap in the yard.' Bill grunts. He is fixing
himself a sandwich.

The Grahams eat sandwiches most days. The only
exception is the last Sunday of the month, when Mandy
defrosts a chicken. Bill zips up his anorak, crams his feet
into a pair of Crocs and drives to the Chicken Out at the
end of the road where he picks up some mash, peas and
cornbread. They eat the meal in silence, the TV tuned to a
John Wayne film.

A week passes. Then one day Mandy hears the doorbell

ring.

'I'll get it,' she shouts to Bill, who has his headphones on. He is watching the baseball, eyes deep inside the television screen.

A young man stands on the front step. He is chubby, with rounded shoulders and a head of tight brown curls. A questioning tilt on the sides of his dark eyes gives him a foreign look. Mandy looks at his hands, checking for any leaflets, but he is only holding a cell phone and a map.

'We're not Jehovah,' Mandy says, her fingers firm around the doorknob.

The man shakes his head.

'I rang last week. I think I spoke to your husband. You advertised a room for rent and I would like to see it,' he says, his foot already inside the door.

She can't place the accent and then she spots his shoes. He's wearing red Nike trainers. They look brand new. She narrows her eyes; she's seen a similar pair on QVC, top of the range, at least ninety bucks.

'Oh, the room! Yes, we got a room all right.' Mandy moves forward, her girth blocking the front door while she tries to remember the last time she hoovered the room in the basement.

He stands close and she can smell the aftershave steaming off his neck.

'You just wait here. I'll call my husband.'

'Bill,' she hollers. 'We got a lodger.'

The young man smiles and extends his hand.

'Hi, my name is Yousef. Yousef Kemal.'

She's not heard such a name before, but confused by his outstretched hand and aware that she's still in her pyjama bottoms and Bill's old, washing-machine-shrunk fleece, she nods and says, 'Mildred Graham. But call me Mandy.'

'Mandy,' he repeats. 'My favourite singer, Barry Manilow, wrote a song about you.' He grins.

Mandy's unsure whether to return the compliment, but she doesn't know any songs with Yousef in them. Yousef. She can't pin the geography or the flag behind the name.

'We'll call you Youz, if that's OK. Sits more comfortably on the tongue,' Bill says, slapping Yousef on the back.

'So, what do you think?' Mandy whispers to Bill, while the young man is checking out the room.

'Seems a good enough chap. He works down at Georgetown, doing research of some sort. Student visa, so he's kosher,' Bill says, pocketing the first month's deposit in crisp hundred-dollar bills.

Yousef reappears.

'May I see the kitchen please?' He stands aside respectfully, as Mandy leads the way to the sunroom that doubles as a kitchen.

Years ago, when Bill was still agile around the house, he'd cleared one wall, fixed the shelves and installed the plumbing for the fridge, the dishwasher and the hob.

'This way you look out and see the kid playing in the yard,' he told Mandy.

'This cupboard can be yours,' Mandy says to Yousef,

pointing vaguely in the direction of the cupboard nearest to the door. She is making up the rules as she goes along. 'And I'll clear the bottom shelf of the freezer and the fridge. And yes, don't use the dishwasher after seven p.m. It makes a hell of a noise.'

Yousef shakes his head. 'No freezer for me, Mrs Mandy. I only cook fresh.'

'Suit yourself.' Mandy shrugs. 'We only cook on Sundays.'

It takes him three days to transfer his belongings from the motel to his new accommodation.

'Looks like he's setting up home,' Bill says.

Mandy notes down each item as it enters her house.

'Shouldn't it be in reverse?' Bill asks. 'Shouldn't you be making an inventory of what we've got, so when he leaves, we got an idea that he's not made off with our stuff?'

'We got nothing worth taking,' Mandy replies.

She drags the beanbag to the front door and carefully writes down each item on a notepad, watching as Yousef unloads his luggage from the hired minivan. She mentions the following:

1.   A blue checked comforter
2.   Velvet slippers
3.   2 Samsonite suitcases
4.   A black lacquer tray inlaid with a mother-of-pearl stork design
5.   Herb pots in a wooden crate and two bags of tomatoes and red onions

'What's that?' She points to a brown ceramic pot with a

cone-shaped lid that Yousef is cradling in his arms like a baby.

'This is a tagine.' He spells out the word slowly. T-A-G-I-N-E.

'It is Moroccan. I use it to cook lamb with chickpeas and apricots. Do you like chickpeas, Mandy?'

'Not really,' Mandy says. 'Chickpeas give me gas.'

On Sunday, Mandy remembers they have a lodger in the house, and she forces herself out of bed. The clock by her bedside says eleven and there is noise in the kitchen. She reaches for her sweatpants and then, changing her mind, pulls on her JCPenney jeans. The waistband cuts into her stomach, but at least she looks decent. Putting some lipstick onto her mouth and dabbing powder on her chin she enters the kitchen.

And there he stands, an apron tied around his rotund belly, busy cracking eggs into a bowl, stirring it with a spatula.

Hey, this is my space, Mandy almost shouts out. Instead, she opens a cupboard and reaches for her stash of Mrs Fields soft baked cookies. She likes dunking them in her morning coffee.

'Try my pancakes,' Yousef says.

'What's that brown thing?' She points to the brown twig in his hand.

'It's a vanilla pod.' He waves it under her nose. She steps back. The smell reminds Mandy of the perfume counter at Macy's.

Whistling under his breath, Yousef snaps open an aluminium box and pours two drops of rose-coloured liquid from a glass vial into the mixture.

Mandy edges closer to get a better look. Rows of glass bottles stand tightly wedged together. Each bottle filled to the brim with different-coloured powders, nuts, and liquid.

A spice rack. She used to have one of those, hanging just above the hob. Paprika and rock salt and Cajun spice mix, rosemary, thyme. Even goddamn verbena.

How she'd loved cooking the drumsticks, coating them with honey and cornflour, then leaning out the window, yelling at the kid to come in and eat.

She rings her daughter, 'Hey, Abigail, guess what your dad and I had for brunch?'

'Let me see. Pork scratchings and an Oreo milkshake?' Abigail's voice is impatient.

'No sir. We had pancakes. Proper home-cooked ones with fresh squeezed vanilla and roses. The whole thing was like a garden growing inside my mouth. That Youz sure got magic in his fingers.'

They begin to look forward to Yousef's return from work each evening. He comes home, his arms loaded with groceries. He's been to the Korean store.

'So much cheaper than Safeway,' he tells them. 'And you get fresh parsley, apricots and even Medjool dates.' He is smiling as he goes down to his room to change.

When he comes back up, he is wearing a loose blue silk tunic that reaches his ankles and carrying his tagine.

'Tonight I make you some lamb tagine. The lamb so tender it will melt in your mouth.'

He kisses his fingertips, making loud smacking noises that frighten the Grahams.

They push their couch nearer to the kitchen door so they can catch the aromas that drift in.

Mandy wanders into the kitchen, watching his hands as they chop, slice and purée.

'You use a lot of garlic,' she observes. 'And way too many tomatoes.'

Yousef's hands are busy stirring a pot in which the tomatoes and the meat dance around in a thick broth.

Her mouth waters.

He scoops the food into small orange terracotta bowls and carries it to them on his lacquer tray with its mother-of-pearl storks.

Bill points to his ham sandwich and Mandy slaps her stomach to show how full she is. But they give in. 'I quite like his foreign food,' Bill confides to Mandy at night. 'It tastes kind of homey.'

Sometimes, Yousef comes home early and sits with them, sharing their couch.

'You guys watch a lot of TV,' he says, and looks away when news comes on of soldiers marching through towns. The houses blow up on the screen like a Fourth of July firework display.

'Are you from those parts?' Bill asks.

'Yes.' He hesitates before continuing. 'But one day my

wife and child will be here and we will all be full-time Americans like you.' He bows his head and shuts his eyes. 'Inshallah,' he whispers.

'Interstellar,' Mandy repeats after him, making the sign of a cross.

He grins and Mandy notices his teeth are Hollywood white and perfect, or maybe it is the contrast with his skin, which, in the lamp light with the curtains drawn, looks coffee brown.

While Yousef's at the university, Mandy likes prowling around among his things.

'Just going down to check on the boiler,' she says to Bill.

Bill grunts and reaches for his pills. His back is giving him trouble and he spends much of the day stretched out on the sofa, a hot-water bottle cushioning his lower spine, his face turned to the television screen, like a child gazing at the moon.

It is an effort for Mandy to climb down the stairs. She grips the banister and pauses at the bottom tread to catch her breath.

She knocks on the door, just to make sure, and enters. The room smells different. A lit incense stick presses its orange nub against the windowpane. She holds the incense stick under her nose and sneezes. It smells of jasmine. It could be a fire hazard, she thinks, and snuffs it out. Velvet slippers wait quietly at the foot of the bed and the comforter is folded in two. She lifts the pillow, plumps it and then presses it against her cheek.

A flash of colour under the bed catches her eye. She bends down and pulls out a small orange rug, rolled up tight. It reminds her of Abigail's yoga mat. She unrolls it. Nestling inside is a small book. She flicks through the pages with their swirly and curly alphabet.

Just as she's about to put it away, a photo of a young woman slips out of the book. A green scarf covers the woman's head. The small child she's holding in her arms gazes unsmiling at the camera.

Mandy walks to the window and holds the photo up to the light. She sees Yousef in the defiant thrust of the little girl's chin and the brown curls that cover her head like a crown.

That night, with Bill snore-deep in sleep beside her, Mandy gets up and opens her underwear drawer, lifts the purple Leonidas box, prises open the lid and takes out a photo. She takes it with her to the bathroom, locks the door, flicks down the toilet seat, sits on it and stares at the picture.

Seasons turn. The trees in the backyard slowly strip off their leaves. Mandy hauls the electric blanket from the garage and tucks it around Bill's lap as he sits watching the commercials on TV.

She offers to buy Yousef a coat.

'That jacket of yours.' She shakes her head. 'No good for our American winter.'

He tells her he's from the mountains; he's used to the cold.

'It will be Christmas soon,' Mandy says. She can't make

up her mind whether she likes or dislikes this fact. 'I suppose you'll be staying, so I'll get a Christmas tree from Home Depot.'

'No going home this year,' Yousef says. 'But I can't wait to show my daughter the Christmas lights. You Americans know how to put on a good show.' His face beams.

Mandy squeezes his hand.

'We will make sure you're not homesick.'

There is talk of turkey, of stuffing it with dates. 'It will be a good change,' Yousef assures Mandy.

'Your daughter Abigail, she will love it.'

'She is vegetarian and she may not be coming home,' Mandy says.

He raises his eyebrows. 'Not coming home for Christmas? She doesn't want to drive around and see the lights with you?'

'She's a businesswoman, very busy,' Mandy says and changes the subject. 'Now tell me, are you sure you'll be able to cook the turkey?'

That evening Yousef asks for Mandy's help in peeling some potatoes. He wants to make a Spanish frittata.

'My little girl, her name is Miriam. It's her favourite.'

There is something shy and proud in his confession. Mandy is curious. She leans forward.

'Where exactly are your folks, Youz?'

He shrugs and says it is a little place on a big map. The name won't mean anything to her.

'Is it where the fighting is?' Mandy says, showing off her

39

radio-heard knowledge.

Yousef's lips shrink into a thin line.

'The fighting is everywhere, Mrs Mandy. We just choose not to see it.'

There is a hissing sound as the oil burns in the frying pan and sets off the smoke alarm. The frittata is burnt but Yousef doesn't seem to notice.

'The world is cruel, Mrs Mandy.'

'Life is cruel,' she agrees and starts buttering the bread.

And then a week before Christmas, Mandy sees Yousef in the backyard, the phone pressed to his ear while his free hand dives inside his trouser pocket to pull out a packet of Marlboros.

'I didn't know Youz smoked,' she says to her husband as she stands at the window watching her lodger pace up and down the hard grey patch of bare lawn.

Bill leans towards her and whispers, 'We mustn't forget he's foreign. That type always got a lot of light and shade in them.'

The change is immediate. Yousef hurries down to his room when he comes home from work. The cheerful waving stops. The 'How is your back today, Bill?' conversations halt. The kitchen no longer hums to the sound of his cooking.

One day Mandy finds him microwaving a packet of macaroni cheese.

'Hey, no bad news from home, I hope?' Mandy keeps her voice cheerful.

Yousef frowns at her and she's not sure if it's a film of water clouding his eyes or just her cataract playing up.

'You won't understand.' His voice is flat, without emotion.

He goes down to his room and stays there.

Two days pass and he's still in his room. At night, voices float up through the floorboards to reach Mandy's anxious ear.

'That boy is in trouble,' she tells her husband.

'Shall we call a doctor?' Bill's eyes are frightened. 'Does he even have health insurance? Is he a terrorist?'

They are old. They have worries of their own.

The next day Mandy drags herself down the front step, gets into the car and drives off to the shops.

When Mandy enters Yousef's room she finds him slumped against the pillows. Dark shadows smudge his eyes and a book lies face down on his chest.

'What's wrong, Youz?' she asks. She's holding a bowl in her hands.

He tells her his daughter is in hospital with an infection in her lungs.

'I feel helpless, so far from her. My only child. It's not right.' Yousef's words fade. His accent thickens. 'She is in a refugee camp in Lebanon. No good doctors there.'

'Lebanon?' Mandy looks puzzled. 'Is that near Africa?'

'Oh my God.' Yousef turns his head to the wall and there is a catch in his voice.

'There is a big world outside this house, Mrs Mandy.

Please pay attention to it.'

'I will. I will,' she promises, sitting on the side of his bed. She lifts the bowl and wedges it firmly between her thighs. Her right hand fishes out the spoon from her T-shirt pocket.

She clears her throat. 'Yousef Kemal' – she calls him by his full name – 'Yousef Kemal, you must not give up. You must eat this so you get strong. Strong enough to bring your family home. To America.' She tilts his chin towards her and scoops a spoon up to his mouth, not stopping until the bowl is glistening white and empty.

Yousef's face softens. He smiles.

'Very tasty. Did you make this? I thought you Americans don't know how to cook.'

'This chicken soup was the kid's favourite,' Mandy says. She is blinking hard and the words rush out.

'Abigail likes this? You told me she's vegetarian.' He knows all about Abigail.

Mandy shakes her head. 'No, no, not her. It was my son Jamie's favourite. I fed him a bowl every day to strengthen his bones.'

The questions come thick and fast. Yousef sits up, his back pressed against the blue gingham headboard, his eyes alert.

Mandy lowers her head and carefully places the empty bowl on the table.

'There was an accident in the swimming pool at school. He was on life support at Chantilly Medical for four months.

He was only six.' Her lips curl into a snarl. 'The lifeguard was sick that day, but still they went ahead with the swimming. The assholes.' She spits out the last word and turns to Yousef, tears like uneven footsteps running down her cheeks. 'We adopted Abigail after he died. She never met her brother.'

She pauses and looks at Yousef to check if he's understood her words. He nods and she continues.

'I hated cooking after he died.'

Her hand lies on the comforter. Yousef entwines his fingers through hers.

'Please don't cry, Mrs Mandy. There is a God somewhere beyond the edge of darkness. He is watching over our children.'

My Mother's Twelfth Suitor

For her eightieth birthday, I buy my mother a red wheelchair. She chooses the model from a catalogue and is won over when the small print says the wheels are assembled in England not China. 'That does it,' she says. 'It's British. It won't let me down.'

'It's better than Dad's. More nimble.' I jerk my chin towards my father's ungainly black wheelchair parked in front of the lounge window, where it sits, like a large toad blocking out the light.

Slowly, insidiously my parents have started competing with each other in collecting the accoutrements of old age. Walking sticks, folding stools, walking frames, they graduate from one to the other with the glee of a child learning to walk again.

'Mine is solid English. Yours looks like it was made in the Soviet Union and we all know what happened to that country.' Mother tut tuts while my father chuckles and says all he's interested in is getting from A to B and back to A again.

My mother has arthritic knees. Her red wheelchair is an aeroplane in which I whiz her in and out of doctors' rooms and X-ray labs, Indian grocery stores and parking lots. Today I'm driving her across town to see an orthopaedist who can help to halt the sound of her bones grinding to ash. Mother sits next to me, round like a knitting ball. Bright lipsticked mouth and forehead smeared with Tiger balm.

We're talking about marriages and husbands. She's speaking about my father without saying his name.

'Highly overrated, this marriage business.' She pats the handbag on her lap like a pet cat.

'Why did you get married then?' I challenge her. It's a stupid question really. She is eighty and has been married for almost sixty years. This is no time for new beginnings.

She leans forward, fiddling with the knobs on the dashboard and raises the heating up a notch, until the air inside the car is a fug of warmth.

'It's June for heaven's sake, Ma.' I wind down the window.

There is silence. My mother is thinking.

'I had twelve suitors,' she announces at the traffic lights. 'One committed suicide and ten stayed unmarried, but there was one who got away that I quite fancied.'

Car horns honk as traffic lights turn from red to green but I stay still, my foot like a stone on the brake pad.

'You're kidding?' I stare at her, my mouth open, seeing her through the twelve suitors' eyes. I imagine her slender hipped with dimpled cheeks and long lashed eyes.

'His name was Bansal. He was tall. He smoked cigarettes and wrote Persian poetry on weekends.'

'He sounds cool', I say betraying my dad who spent his life hiding behind his office files.

She nods. 'He was one of a kind.'

We arrive at the hospital. The orthopaedist has American teeth-white pearls strung along his pink gums and a mop of sandy hair he keeps pushing back with a languid hand. In another life, he might have been a cruise ship crooner belting out Frank Sinatra. But for now he must pass his days tending to the knees of geriatric patients who have been careless in their youth. He scrunches up his eyes, bringing up the image of my mother's knees on the screen. The ravaged bones shine through.

'You've left it too late,' he says shaking his head.

'What about cortisone injections?' I pipe up.

He waves this away. His gaze floats back to the X-ray where my mother's damaged knees glint like a murder weapon.

'Can you see the cartilage there?'

I nod at the ivory coloured blurred shadow on the screen.

'There are several alternatives one could consider but given her age...' he says. 'I could do an arthroscopic washout and debridement or an osteotomy.'

'Stop.' My mother halts him mid-sentence. 'I'll just have to live with these buggers, that's that. Nothing doing'. And with that my mother hauls herself into her wheelchair and taps the arm rest with one red painted finger nail ready for take-off.

We drive home.

'What about this Bansal. The suitor who got away eh.' I want to lighten the mood, make her feel good about herself again.

'The wedding date was set. I was all giddy with delight.' She smiles and touches my arm.

'I was only nineteen remember. People got married young those days.'

She giggles and doesn't seem to mind when we drive past our house, only raising an eyebrow and saying how good it is to talk of icebergs.

'Icebergs? What do you mean?' My mother's mind is going the same way as her knees, I think.

'It's simple really,' she explains. 'We get older and little parts of ourselves fall away, like icebergs floating out of view and suddenly when you think all is lost, you turn a corner and there it is, voilà that little blob of ice you thought you'd never see again. That's how it is with Bansal. He's that little blob that I've just remembered.'

This moment may never come back. I keep driving.

I clear my throat, think of Dad, who's spent his life filling dental cavities, and writing seminar papers on genetics and oral health.

'Well Bansal's loss is Dad's gain. You're so happy together.'

I keep my tone light and bright and turn on the radio where Louis Armstrong is singing about a wonderful world.

'Your father is a good man. He is reliable like a cargo ship but that Bansal he was something else. He was an Italian speedboat.' She narrows her eyes and stares out of the car window.

'So what happened to this speedboat? Why did he leave

47

you on the shore? Didn't he want to be with you?'

'Want is such a big and scary word, isn't it? What we want and what we need are two different animals all together.' She smiles and carries on.

'I met Bansal before the wedding. He came to see me in the park next to my house. We sat on a bench; he held my hand and recited some words from Rumi.' Her eyes are dreamy. 'The wound is the place where the Light enters you, that's what he said. I thought he was being romantic, but he was only preparing me.'

'When did Dad appear?' I ask but she raises her hand.

'Let me finish.'

'Bansal called off the wedding.' Her voice lowers. 'It was such a scandal. He moved to Australia and set up home with a man. I cried and refused to go to college. Bansal wrote to my parents explaining how he didn't want to ruin my life.' There's a faint tremor in her voice. 'I don't have the right mind set for your daughter, he said. Just imagine what a waste of a life.' She sighs.

'I met your Dad six months later. He'd come to my university to do some research. I was waiting at the bus stop one day. It was raining and he offered me a lift.'

That night I dream of my mother and Bansal slow waltzing in the outback. Her knees are round, soft and shiny like a child's. His arm is around her waist. Above them is the sky drunk with a thousand stars.

Cooking Chicken in Kentucky

Peter and Caroline stand together in their hotel room, elbows on the window ledge, staring at the golden fields. They are in a small village outside Calais.

A gunshot followed by loud shouts breaks the stillness. A plume of smoke curls up from a clump of trees bordering the fields. Caroline frowns as she looks at the smoke that briefly hides the sun.

'I hope everything's okay.'

Peter says he'd read in the papers about a refugee colony near the village.

'Don't worry about it,' he says, his fingers brushing the nape of her neck. His voice is a whisper. 'This weekend is about us.'

∞

They drive to Calais to catch the ferry home, stopping at a petrol station to re-fuel. Peter fills up and goes in to pay while Caroline stays in the car. Through the rear-view mirror she spots a group of young men huddled together near the hard shoulder of the motorway. Dark skinned and dressed in shiny tracksuits they look out of place. One of them punches the air with his fist and they scatter in different directions.

The car smells of cheese and cuts of ham, mementoes of their French weekend. Caroline had spent the morning in a

49

frenzy of buying camembert and Bordeaux reds from the farmers' market in the village square. The food packed in shiny brown paper bags fills the back seat. The smell makes her retch and she winds down the windows to let in some fresh air. She feels a headache coming on and dozes off.

They make the ferry just in time.

'Lots of shopping, eh?' The border guard glances at the back seat and flicks through their passports with a yawn.

'Il est notre anniversaire. J'aime beaucoup Le France, aussi ma...' Peter hesitates, searching for the right word.

'Femme,' Caroline finishes his sentence.

'Meilleurs vœux'. The gendarme waves them on.

They reach home after midnight. Peter's back is sore from driving and he wants to go to bed right away.

'Don't worry. I'll do the unpacking,' Caroline says, patting his arm.

∞

In the garage, she fumbles for the light, almost tripping over Peter's golf clubs. Two rounds from the car to the fridge and she is almost done, when she returns one last time for the wine in the boot. A soft thud and a small bundle rolls out of the boot and settles near her feet. Does she scream? She can't remember.

The grey bundle uncurls itself and crouches at her feet. It is a small boy with what she can only describe as PG Tips brown skin and a head of tightly woven curls. He opens his mouth and she sees the gap between his two front teeth.

'Who the hell are you?' She grabs a golf club, waving it like a flag.

He squats on the floor, dusty toes curled against the cold concrete floor. Caroline comes nearer and he raises his arms, covering the top of his head, readying himself for the blow. She is about to run upstairs and shake Peter awake when she stops. How dangerous can he be? A little boy who looks lost and confused. The golf club slips from her hand. Crouching down, one hand pressing his shoulder, she asks, 'Who are you?'

He blinks rapidly and starts rocking back and forth, shivering in his faded blue tracksuit bottom and a striped tee shirt that seems too tight on his body.

A small hoarse voice mumbles something.

Caroline frowns. 'Sorry, I don't understand.'

He sticks out his tongue. It is pale and flecked with white.

She hears his stomach rumble and understands. 'You want food.'

In the kitchen, she quickly cuts him slices of thick white bread, makes him milky tea and pours him water. He eats too quickly, retching once or twice, bringing up the tea. It dribbles down the side of his mouth and neck, a thin brown stream wending its way down his tee shirt.

'Hey, slowly, eat slowly,' she says, glancing towards the stairs to check whether the commotion has woken up Peter.

The boy points to his crotch and she takes him to the downstairs loo. The trickle of his urine rings out feeble and

51

lonely in the silent house. She goes back to the bathroom and flushes the toilet twice, emptying a bottle of Dettol into the bowl.

Afterwards, she takes him into the garden and hands him an old sleeping bag that she spreads in the garden shed.

'Be very quiet,' she tells him as he edges himself inside the sleeping bag. 'Only come out when I tell you.'

Caroline lies awake, staring at the window, willing the daylight to come faster.' She imagines the boy prowling downstairs. His small, sweaty hands running like mice through her things.

∞

Next morning Peter rushes to work and there is no time for explanations. Caroline can't understand why she, sparrow-timid at heart, hasn't confided in him. She calls in sick at the school where she teaches and stands at the kitchen sink staring at the neighbour's house.

The door opens. It is the boy watching her, his dark eyes alert.

'I told you not to come out, until I call you.'

He stands, eyes fixed on her face.

'H-E-L-L-O and G-O-O-D M-O-R-N-I-N-G. Did you sleep well?' She speaks slowly, pronounces each syllable clearly. He doesn't reply.

'Don't be afraid,' She goes up to him and strokes his cheek. He steps back, his index finger rubbing his cheek.

She tries again. 'What is your name?'

'Ali,' the boy whispers finally. 'Name is Ali,' he repeats.

'Like Ali Baba.' She smiles, but he doesn't smile back. He is looking at the fruit bowl piled high with apples.

She points to her stomach, patting it with her palm. 'Hungry?'

He nods.

'You need to brush your teeth first. Have a shower.' Caroline's voice is brisk and teacher-like. The boy stinks of dried sweat and straw.

Ali follows Caroline upstairs, bare feet padding on the carpeted floor. She turns on the shower. He strips and squats on the floor, head buried between his folded arms. The water beats against his skin like rain. His elbows jut out, thin, bony and needy.

She gives him Peter's gym tee shirt and a pair of old shorts. In the bedroom, she hides her pearl necklace under the mattress.

Ali comes down, drowning in his borrowed clothes, his old ones rolled tight against his chest.

He points to the fruit bowl.

She throws him an apple and he lunges forward to catch it and misses. He giggles his face opening up like a flower.

Caroline pats the empty chair beside her.

'Come and sit.'

He sits, swinging his foot, taking quick bites of the fruit.

'How did you end up in my car?'

He doesn't understand her question, so she mimics the motion of driving a car, her hands going round an imaginary steering wheel.

Ali gets up and edges towards the door.

'Don't worry. I won't tell the police.' She takes his elbow and leads him back to the chair.

'Where are you from, Ali?' Caroline asks, pretending as though he's a new boy who's just joined her class.

'Somalia,' he answers. 'In Africa.' His voice has a small American twang.

'That's far away,' Caroline says. 'How did you get in my car? Was it in France?'

Ali nods without looking at her.

'And...?' She prompts.

He sighs and starts speaking. Words spill out haltingly.

'I come in lorry. Lorry with sheep. We hide under the animals.' He screws up his nose. 'Aatch stinking with shit.'

Caroline asks him how long he'd been in the lorry. He holds his fingers up and says four days.

He continues. 'We wait near the petrol station and the driver get angry and screams, get out, get out fast.' Ali snaps his fingers.

'Everybody run. I see your car. You sleeping. I hide inside.'

She listens rapt. It's like hearing a fairy-tale.

'Your mother? Was she in the lorry also?' Caroline wants to make sure the boy is not alone. She pictures his mother roaming the streets, calling his name; her eyes helpless with panic.

Ali folds his arms, looks at his feet. He frowns.

'No mother.'

'You speak good English.'

He shrugs. 'I go to UN school in camp.'

Her mobile on the kitchen counter vibrates as Peter's number flashes. Caroline ignores it but Ali's arm shoots out and he grabs her phone. Eyes narrowed, his thumb runs over the screen. 'You have iPhone.' He looks at her approvingly.

'It's just a phone,' Caroline says, 'In fact let's call your mother.' She looks at him expectantly, her fingers ready to punch in the numbers.

Ali says something in a language she doesn't understand.

'English please,' Caroline adopts her teacher's voice. 'We are in England now.'

'Mother has no phone,' Ali replies, switching to English. He rubs away at his eyes with the heel of his palm.

'Where is your father? I can let him know you are safe.'

This time Ali answers straight away, repeating almost parrot fashion, lines he has memorised.

'My father is dead. He was soldier. And my mother.' Ali's hands fold into fists and he places them flat on the table like a sleeping animal. 'My mother very ill. She sits inside the camp and prays to god. My mother wants me to be doctor. If I stay in Somalia, I become soldier. I die like my father. Go to England she says. Live.'

He begins to cry, dry sobs jiggling his shoulders.

'Don't cry, please don't cry,' Caroline stands over him, wringing her hands. She squeezes his arm and hands him a

55

Kleenex. He blows his nose and throws the used tissue on the floor.

After a while, the sobs die out and he looks around the kitchen.

'You are rich.' He states it like a fact.

Caroline feels her cheeks go warm. 'We get by. We have no children so we can save.'

Her fridge is stuffed with French cheese and wine and organic fruits. Hers is a rich life but sitting next to him, she suddenly feels poor.

'You have no girl. No boy?' Ali's eyebrows go up in surprise.

'I have plenty of god children, nephews, nieces,' Caroline explains. Her voice turns loud and sunny. She changes the subject.

'You must be hungry. Let me make you a sandwich.'

She busies herself slicing the bread, slathering it with jam.

A small swell of disgust rises in her as she watches him stuff the bread into his mouth. There is something naked and ugly in his perpetual hunger.

'Eat slowly. It's not running away,' she says.

She glances at the clock. Soon it will be lunchtime and she can hear Ali's stomach rumble again. Boys had big appetites.

'I am going to cook your food.' Caroline stops herself. She must speak properly so the boy can learn. 'I am going to prepare your lunch. What is your favourite dish?'

'We eat mutton at Eid. My grandfather is killing goat.' His eyes shine at the memory.

'What is your best food?' It's his turn to ask.

Caroline shrugs. 'I don't know. Caesar salad, I guess.'

Ali's face is blank but he swivels in his chair and looks around.

'This is big house. Many people live here.'

'It's not that big,' she corrects him. 'We bought it ages back when prices weren't so ridiculously high. I live here with my husband.'

'Your husband is soldier.' Ali leans towards her, examining her face, eyes narrowed, checking for signs of buried grief.

'Oh no, Peter is an accountant.' She smiles. 'But he is a busy man. I will introduce you to him later.'

'He is not dead. You are lucky woman. Uncle Musa also live here. He works in Kentucky, cooking chicken,' he pronounces the name proudly. 'He said he will give me a job cooking chicken in Kentucky.'

Caroline bursts out laughing. 'How cute is that.' She stops to get her breath back and tells Ali solemnly that the correct name of his uncle's employer is Kentucky Fried Chicken.

∞

Later that morning, while Ali naps, she drives to an unfamiliar part of town with boarded up shops and council flats. A group of Somali women stand at the traffic light, waiting to cross. Their black robes billow in the afternoon breeze.

Caroline rolls down her car window.

'Excuse me. Can you suggest a good butcher that sells mutton?'

The women look at each other and the youngest one, the one with a silver stud in her nose speaks, gesturing with her hands.

Caroline hears them giggle as she drives away.

Back home she downloads the recipe from the computer. The onions make her eyes sting and the pan sputters with oil. She flings open the window, worried the neighbours will complain as the smells of garlic and onion waft out into the London air. The meat tastes like leather and she spits it out before calling Ali, piling soft mounds of rice and mutton on his plate, until he clutches his stomach saying, 'Stop, I can eat no more.'

'Is it good?' she asks.

'Not good like my mother, 'Ali replies.

He passes the second night in the garden shed.

'Don't make a noise,' she warns again, pressing a finger to her lip. 'We don't want to disturb my husband. He get very angry.'

'Your husband call police?' Ali's face twists in fear. She shakes her head and says he is a good man but she needs time before she tells him.

Tomorrow, she tells herself. I promise I will tell Peter tomorrow.

∞

She can't avoid going to work the next morning.

'Make yourself at home,' she tells Ali, bringing out the Tupperware with the left over mutton. She switches on the TV, flicking through the channels until a Disney cartoon comes up.

She tweaks his cheek.

'You're a good boy.' Her hand lingers on his face.

'I'm going to hire a good lawyer, sort your papers out... maybe we can adopt you.'

Ali sitting cross-legged on the sofa, chin cupped in his hands, engrossed in the cartoon doesn't hear her.

Returning home from work, she buys a chocolate cake. It'll be a surprise for Ali. Also a sweetener for Peter as she introduces him to the boy. He will like Ali. Her eyes well up imagining their meeting. Peter sweeping Ali into his arms. 'Someone to fill the silence...' he'll joke, winking at her. Didn't he always say the house could do with the patter of little feet? Hadn't he painted the spare room bright canary yellow in anticipation of children to come? So busy is she drawing up plans she almost crashes into the police car with its flashing lights that's blocking her front door.

Caroline runs inside, her handbag and shopping bag slide from her hand. Peter's in the kitchen, lips clamped tight, white in anger. A police officer is scribbling something in a notebook. Ali stands near them. He is back in his old clothes, his head bowed. He looks up when he sees Caroline, but his eyes are mute.

'Ali,' she whispers, running to him. 'You okay?'

It was the postman. He'd spotted the brown face through the window and called the police.

'We've had a narrow escape. This scoundrel had broken in, trying to make off with our stuff,' Peter says, grabbing her arm.

The police officer agrees. 'He doesn't have any papers on him.'

'You can't do anything to him.' She places a protective hand on Ali's shoulder. 'He is innocent. His uncle works in Kentucky... Ali's a good boy.' Her voice falters and she begins crying, her folded arms pressed tight against her chest.

Peter raises an eyebrow. 'Calm down, Caroline. You're not thinking straight. You've never set eyes on this boy before.'

The policeman turns to Ali.

'Do you know this lady?' He raises his voice. 'Do you know her?'

'I don't know her.' Ali shakes his head and spits on the floor.

∞

They watch the nine o'clock news. There is a special report on the crackdown on illegal immigration.

'We had a narrow escape. Poor faceless mutt. Thank God you were out and all. You should know better,' says Peter reaching for his wine glass. He takes an appreciative sip and smacks his lips. 'Good vintage, this. I'm glad we picked it up over the weekend.'

'He is not a faceless mutt. His name is Ali. All he wants is to have a better life,' Caroline says. Her voice is wobbly as though she were treading water and failing to find a footing.

'You're overreacting, darling. You don't know him.' Peter sighs and reaches out to hold her hand.

Caroline pushes his hand away.

∞

Ali's fingers had grazed hers as he followed the policeman. He whispered words meant for her alone.

'I will work in Kentucky. No worry. I will come and see you.'

Caroline opens the back door and steps outside. Bare feet buried deep in grass, her face upturned to the scatter of stars patrolling the night sky. She lets out a howl.

Be a Soldier

It takes the Chens a long time to reach England. After changing planes in Dubai, they board the Heathrow express to Paddington before catching the 451 National Express to their son's town. The English countryside passes them – a streak of green verges, brown-hatted houses huddled close and blinking neon signs for burgers and sun beds. For much of the way, Mrs Chen dozes, her body folded in an awkward c-shape, arms folded across her chest, her cheek pressed against the grey tinted bus window. Her husband sits straight, shoulders pushed back, his eyes trained on the road. His hands rest lightly on his lap.

The coach stops once at a service station on the motorway but the couple stay in their seats. Mrs Chen rummages through the brown bag lying at her feet and brings out two sweet buns wrapped in cellophane and a packet of sesame nut bars.

'Sure you don't want tea or something. Stretch your legs?' the bus driver asks as he walks down the aisle, bending down to pick up empty crisp packets and discarded newspapers.

'Thank you, but we will drink tea at our son's home,' Mrs Chen replies.

The driver shrugs and looks at them more closely. His eyes narrow.

'Where are you from?'

'Guangzhou, Flat 14 E, Sun yet Sen Road.' Mrs Chen's voice rises at the end.

'We have our British visa,' her husband adds.

The driver smiles. His mouth is crowded with uneven pointy teeth that give him a faintly canine air.

'Next thing you'll be telling me what kind of noodles you're having for tea,' he says, shaking his head.

The Chens are the first to disembark when the coach finally reaches the depot. Outside the day lies curtained behind a mist of fine drizzle. It's still summer but they've travelled north and the people wear sweaters and scarves, their faces blue grey in the afternoon light. Mrs Chen pulls out a red woollen scarf from her tote and knots it around her neck.

Their son stands under the bus shelter, hands jammed in his pockets, swaying back and forth on the balls of his feet, just as his mother remembers.

'Zheng still looks like a kid.' She turns to her husband. He nods. 'But remember he is a teacher now. A grown man. Soon to be father.' He grins and touches her shoulder lightly.

Zheng spots them and runs towards them. The open flaps of his checked jacket move like wings of a bird. Breathless, he bends down, kisses the top of his mother's head, and extends his hand to his father, who ignoring it, enfolds him in a hug.

'Three years eh, Pa? Was that the last time?' Zheng asks, moving out of the embrace. He removes his glasses and wipes the lens with a handkerchief that peeps from his jacket pocket. Mrs Chen notices the pink ridge on his nose where his glasses had been.

'It feels like a long lifetime,' the father says. Mrs Chen stands still, examining the tips of her shoes, waiting her turn to hug the son. She had bought the shoes in the Haizhu Wholesale Market in preparation for the long journey. They were black because she didn't want them to get dirty even though her husband had assured her that rich countries like England were dirt free. 'All we have to worry about is the rain.' They packed three types of umbrellas to cope. One was a large golf sized presented to Mr Chen on retirement, its striped blue and red fabric emblazoned with the company logo of a soaring eagle clutching a gold globe and two smaller neat folding ones. Mrs Chen didn't want her English daughter in law to think they had come unprepared. She remembers the girl's name now as she follows the father and son to the car.

'How is Martha?' She pronounces the name carefully. She'd road tested the sound with her next door neighbour, Mrs Dolly, an old Indian lady who wore chiffon saris and pearls and whose son worked as an IT something in New Jersey. Mrs Dolly was familiar with Western names. She told Mrs Chen how to say the name: 'Maartha... not Malta.' It had taken four lessons to get it right.

'She's so excited to see you, Ma. Sorry she couldn't come, but in her state, she gets tired easily.' He calls Mrs Chen, Ma and not the stiff Mother with which he first greeted her. She pinches his arm. Her little Zheng all grown up with his own wife and a child on its way. Her eyes well up.

It's a small house like a cereal box placed on the side of a road. Next to it, as far as Mrs Chen can see stretch similar cornflake box shaped houses. A patch of green with two empty swings lies at the front. The baby can play here, she thinks as her son opens the front door.

'Welcome to my world.' Zheng bows and extends his arm in a flourish that takes in the blue striped sofa and the wall mounted Sony television. Underneath the television is a narrow shelf crowded with pictures. Mrs Chen can't spot herself in any of them. So busy is she taking in the details, she doesn't see the girl standing by the kitchen table holding a mug in her hands.

'Meet Martha,' Zheng says, a protective arm around the girl's thin, rounded shoulders.

Martha smiles, puts down her mug, comes forward and gives Mrs Chen a peck on the cheek. 'I'm so happy to meet you at last, Mrs Chen,' Martha says. She takes a wrapped packet from the table and presses it into her hands.

'A little welcome gift.'

Mrs Chen tears the silvery shiny paper and frowns when she sees the pink slippers.

'Why shoes? In China we give fruit or flowers.' She speaks to her son in Mandarin. 'Your feet will be snug and warm in these,' Zheng replies in English. 'They are from Marks and Spencer. The best department store in England.'

It's Mrs Chen's turn to give her daughter in law a gift.

65

She dips her hand inside her bag and pulls out a red silk pouch.

'For you and your baby to be. Open it please.' Her eyes shine in excitement as she watches Martha pull the gold cord. Out slips a jade statue of a smiling rotund Buddha.

'Thank you, it's so cute and plump just like my belly,' Martha giggles.

'It will bring good luck to your life.' Mrs Chen beams. Taking the statue from her daughter in law's hand, she places it on the mantelpiece right in the middle.

'Let's all have some tea.' Zheng's voice is loud and bright.

'Do you have green tea?' Mr Chen asks. 'Of course, Pa,' Zheng replies. 'Went to Chinatown yesterday to get Ying Kee especially for you. Martha and I prefer PG Tips.'

'PG Tips?' Mrs Chen wrinkles her nose. 'I don't understand.'

'Andrew means tea.' Martha laughs.

'Andrew?' Mr Chen repeats. 'Who is Andrew?'

Zheng's cheeks turn pink as he explains to his parents that he had adopted a new English name. 'Only for official purposes. It's easier for everyone...,' his voice dips down. Mrs Chen's shoulders sag on hearing this.

'But Zheng is such an easy and sweet name...' she begins but her husband brings his finger to his mouth. 'Remember we are guests here.'

They hear the kettle hissing.

Mr Chen picks up a photo from the shelf and examines it carefully, his thumb running over the tortoiseshell frame.

66

He turns to Martha. 'Nice wedding. Sorry we couldn't attend. Work difficulties.'

Mrs Chen knows better. They didn't have enough savings to purchase the airline tickets, but there was no point in confessing this shame to the foreign looking girl who sat before them, her legs spread out, her pregnant belly moving up and down with her breath, smiling at them with such a puzzled look.

Mrs Chen realises she has to become friends with this girl who has anchored her son to this foreign soil. Held him down so tight that that he has forgotten to swim back to the shore.

She sits next to Martha and holds her hand just as a mother would.

'Dear Martha. So nice to meet you finally.'

'Same here, Mrs Chen,' Martha replies, shifting away. It's a slight, imperceptible movement, but Mrs Chen notices it all the same. Her shoulders stiffen.

'Please call me Ma. I'm Zheng's ma, so I'm your Ma too.'

Martha smiles. 'Oh but I do have a mother. She lives in Costa del Sol. She'll visit me next summer.'

Their wedding was quick. Zheng had rung them, telling them about the English girl who had stolen his heart. It was the British way. Mrs Chen knew that. See something you like and snatch it like fruit from a tree. Hadn't they done the same with Hong Kong?

Instead of a red qipao, Maratha wore a white dress and Zheng's work colleagues threw a party in the local pub. No nine courses of stuffed Hokkaido Crab Legs, Peking duck and braised Abalone for her only son. Instead, they had feasted on meat pies and beer.

Mrs Chen sighs.

'So how long to go now?' She asks even though a quick glance shows her that the baby was ready to drop like a ripe mango. 'Please come and look after her,' Zheng had begged them over the telephone. Hearing the pleading in his voice, the Chens forgave him his hasty marriage to a foreigner; they took out their life savings and crossed the seven seas.

'You should be drinking Chinese tea and plenty of rest,' Mrs Chen tells Martha, Landing her a cup. 'Put your legs up and wear a sweater. No point catching cold with baby blooming inside you like a flower.'

'Andrew knows I don't like green tea.' Martha makes a face. 'I'll have the biscuit.' Mrs Chen flinches when she hears the name Andrew. Her son was rubbing himself away but she is determined his child, her grandson wouldn't do the same.

'She's not used to our flavours.' Zheng was leaping to his wife's defence.

A memory floats before Mrs Chen. She was a new bride and her mother in law, old Mrs Chen, stood over her, her thin long fingers jabbing her shoulder. 'This is the way the soup is cooked in our house. Not your peasant Guizhou way.' Her husband had stayed mute like a fish, hiding behind the newspaper. Old Mrs Chen, god bless her departed soul, ruled the house like Genghis Khan. She must do the same if she wanted the Chen name to carry on. Make sure her traditions flourished in this dull grey corner of England.

Mrs Chen sets about transforming her son's life. She gets up early, wraps the apron around her boyish gaunt hips and carefully places jars of preserved ginger root, pickled fish eggs and roasted tripe on the shelves. She had eaten these during her own pregnancy and what a wonderful son she had produced. True her wishes that he become a wealthy banker in Hong Kong married to a mainland girl hadn't materialised, but here he is, happy and healthy, an about-to-be father.

'She's not eating right kind of food. Always cheese sandwiches and orange juice that swims in sugar,' she confides in her husband at night. Wide-awake they watch the rain tapping against the Velux window on the roof.

'It's her baby. Maybe she knows best. Why interfere?' Mr Chen says, turning on his side with a grunt.

'How will she know what's good for a Chinese baby? She's never set foot in China,' Mrs Chen prods her husband on the shoulder, but he is fast asleep.

Not her, she spends the night plotting ways to make the pregnancy go right.

The next day, Mrs Chen throws away the digestive chocolate biscuits and bulk supplies of Walkers salt and vinegar crisps from the kitchen cupboard above the sink.
'Not good for the baby boy,' she tells Martha, head shaking vehemently. 'He will get hiccups and tummy ache.'

Martha lies on the sofa, one hand resting on her belly, the other holding the television remote. 'How do you know it's a boy? I could be having triplets and all girls too, ginger haired and freckly like me.'

'Only sons in the Chen family tree,' Mrs Chen's voice is defiant.

Martha rises from the sofa and goes to her bedroom. 'You know nothing about our English ways. Your mumbo jumbo won't work on me, Mrs Chen,' she says, slamming the door shut.

Mrs Chen lights two joss sticks in the living room to purify the atmosphere of any rancour.

Zheng brings fish and chips for their Friday night dinner. 'It's the national favourite dish,' he says, unwrapping the newspaper packaging and sliding the fish onto a plate.

'The batter is too salty,' Mrs Chen declares. She pushes away the fish after just one bite.

Later that evening Zheng prepares his mother a bowl of chicken corn soup, the spring onion shredded finely, just the way she likes it. Mrs Chen smiles. Where her daughter in law had sliced open her heart with a butcher's knife, her son had folded it like a flower and handed it back to her.

'Ma, be gentle with your advice,' Zheng reminds Mrs Chen as he leaves for work every morning, his forehead creases in worry. 'Girls here don't like to be ordered. It's not the English way.'

'Don't her parents care? Don't they want to look after her?'

Zheng explained that Martha's parents were divorced and had busy lives of their own.

Mrs Chen rubs her chin as she considers this. 'Poor girl. I must make up for their neglect.' She hands Zheng his packed lunch, his favourite steamed sesame buns. 'You go now and earn money for your child.'

Every morning Mrs Chen tiptoes into her son's room, bends over her sleeping daughter in law and whispers Buddhist prayers into her ear. Her deepest wish is that the child be born Chinese, with low hooded eyes and skin the colour of a moon lit magnolia flower.

'Let's go for a walk,' Mrs Chen suggests one sunny day.

'I suppose it'll do me good,' Martha mumbles. She wags her finger. 'Let's just walk.'

They go to the park, Mrs Chen slows down so she is walking side by side with Martha who curls her lip as though in pain. Her feet have swelled during pregnancy and her shoes pinch.

'Let's turn back,' she says.

But Mrs Chen is having none of it. 'Walk barefoot and feel the energy of the earth.'

Martha points to the black tarmacked road and says the only thing she'll feel would be broken beer bottles and syringes.

'The baby needs fresh air. No good watching television all day. The boy will be born wearing glasses.' Mrs Chen says. She brings up her hands to her face, forming two circles with the thumb and index finger and presses them

71

around her eyes and sticks out her tongue. The image makes them laugh.

'You're a wise old soul. I suppose you're doing the best for the baby,' Martha says, bending down to give her a quick hug.

She winces and clutches her tummy. 'I just felt the baby move.'

Mrs Chen presses her ear against her daughter in law's belly. 'I can hear the baby singing in this beautiful park.' Tears flood her eyes.

'I hate this park. What's beautiful about it?' Martha says. 'Look at all these houses crowded round'.

Mrs Chen points out the tall chestnut trees in the distance and the rhododendron bushes glittering with purple-headed flowers. 'In Guangzhou, to live near a park is a dream. My building has twenty-five floors and no trees everywhere I look. The only way to catch the sky is through my bathroom window.'

Mrs Chen stops. She would've liked to tell Martha that she spent most mornings in Guangzhou, sitting on a plastic stool in her bathroom, craning her neck, trying to read the sky and the passing clouds. Her husband was busy too, retired he had converted Zheng's old bedroom into a home office. He was making secret plans for their retirement, he told her, when she questioned why he wouldn't let her dust the room. One day she snuck into the room and found on the desk Japanese magazines of naked schoolgirls with knee high socks.

'Be happy, Martha. New life growing inside your belly. Look at those trees. See how proud and tall they are. Like soldiers, eh. You learn to be like a soldier also. Keep marching on,' Mrs Chen says, holding Martha's hand.

Martha's waters break one afternoon when Zheng was still at work and Mr Chen had taken the bus to the nearest shopping mall. Mrs Chen was in the kitchen peeling onions when she heard the scream. She rushed to Martha's bedroom to find her doubled over with pain. A puddle of water lay at her feet, staining the carpet.

'Ma, help me, Ma,' Martha had shouted grabbing Mrs Chen's arm.

Afterwards, back home in Guangzhou, Mrs Chen would shake her head reliving the moment and marvelling at her bravery. 'How did I do it? She asked her neighbour, Mrs Dolly. 'How did I drive an English car on English roads to St. George's hospital?' She had bundled the sobbing girl onto the back seat that she covered with towels and a folded duvet. At the last minute, she had rushed to the living room, grabbed the jade Buddha statue from its shrine, and pressed it into Martha's hands. 'Remember, you be soldier now,' she told her.

While Martha gasped out directions to the hospital, Mrs Chen jumped two red lights and one false turn to the left, thankful that this was a small sleepy English town with well-behaved cars. She could never have done this in big, booming, Hong Kong.

Only after Martha was whisked into the maternity ward did Mrs Chen relax. She rang her son.

'Come quickly,' she said. 'The time has come to greet your new born.' She paused and continued excitedly, tripping over the words. 'Martha held my hand and called me Ma.' She squealed in delight.

Benjamin Hanjong Chen was born at 8 pm that night, weighing six pounds six. The first person to hold him was his grandmother who noted with delight that although a sliver of ginger hair topped his head, his skin was the colour of moon lit magnolia and his eyes, the bearer of his soul were perfect almond shaped Chinese eyes. No one would ever mistake him for an English man.

Mrs Chen wept tears of joy.

Days by the Sea

Ma wants to end her days by the sea. Away from the city where people loiter on the streets, gauze bandages wrapped around their noses to block the stench of effluents pouring from factories. Away from dogs, sniffing their way to food among the piles of marigold garlands discarded on the temple steps. Away from the queues of gaunt-boned women outside the Government approved stores, waiting to collect their daily quota of bread, salt and sugar. It is a world she doesn't want to belong to anymore.

But the People's Progress Party (established 1879) will not let her go. There are security concerns. Old enmities bloom like an itch. Pale long envelopes addressed to Ma arrive at Suite 105 of the shining chrome and glass building that serves as the Party headquarters. Nestling among the folds of paper are soft silk pouches filled with arsenic. One day a bouquet of red roses lands on her desk, a scorpion's sting hiding between the petals.

'We can't allow you to leave. You are still the honourable head of our Party,' says the Minister of Home Security. He sits across her, a small man with a balding head and elbows propped on her desk. His lips are stained orange, a result of chewing betel nut over the years.

'The people are angry, Ma. They are also hungry. They want to know why when the fields are overflowing with crop; there is no rice to fill their belly. They want the truth,' he continues, eyes flickering with meaning.

She shrugs. 'It's nothing to do with me. Remember we are in the Opposition. Someone else rules this country and as for the bloody Truth.' Ma plays with the word. 'Such an ugly word that. We use it so much.' She snaps her fingers-a dry sound ricocheting between the walls. 'One day it becomes just another word. Meaningless. Do you know any other such words, Minister?' She arches an eyebrow and looks at him.

'No Ma, I don't, but I read newspapers. Sometimes I watch television too and our people are restless. They are quick to blame and they take a long time to forget.' He scratches his chin and glances at his Swiss watch. The leather strap is worn, he'll need a replacement soon, he thinks.

Her lips fold in a thin smile. 'The fickle mob. Isn't that what Shakespeare calls them?' The Minister bows his head. He is only a high school graduate and such literary allusions are lost on him.

Once upon a time, she could have clapped her hands and made him disappear. Those days are gone. She is no longer in power and her reach is limited. The Minister moistens his orange mouth with his tongue and continues. 'Don't worry, Ma. The masses are like stubborn children. Soon they will realise that this new leader is no good. They will come around and the People's Progress Party will rule again. It will take time. Until then it is best you don't expose yourself to undue danger.' His fingertips touch each other to form an imaginary peak.

She frowns. 'I don't want to be anybody's Ma anymore.'

Her own son had left years back. Sickened by the horse-trading and stench of vote baiting he packed his bags and slipped away to make his fortune in colder climes. He now filed tax returns for rich divorcees and entertained clients in Sushi bars. So she had heard.

'MA.' Her voice capitalizes the letters. It is how the Party projected her at every election. Huge billboards towered over highways, her image in bright technicolour, the sari pallu pulled demurely over her head. Babies crawling over her maternal lap. 'Come, give Mother your vote,' the slogans shrieked. 'She is your saviour.'

Now there is a new leader. A plump-cheeked technocrat returned from America who promises a computer and a toilet in every village hut. He played her at her own game. To think she funded his study at Harvard and nurtured his rise through the party ranks. The next minute he had formed a breakaway coalition of his own. The brat! This was how he repaid her. At the last election, he beat her by a million votes, but gracious in victory had let her keep her cream stucco bungalow, her Mercedes and retinue of lackeys. He even created a title for her, 'Mother-in-charge.'

'You are woven into the moral fabric of our nation,' he smirked, the American twang loud in his voice. She'd flinched from his embrace.

It is time for her to retreat.

A large gilt framed mirror hangs on the wall behind the

Minister's chair. She studies it. Rounded shoulders and a white sari. Her grey-streaked hair hangs in a tired plait. A single ivory bangle dangles on each bare arm, a gift from her late husband.

A simple woman. A woman of the people.

'I have made up my mind. I will be by the sea.' Ma raises her left hand ever so slightly from her lap. With such a gesture, she had sent growing men quivering to their ruin.

The Minister tries one last time.

'At least allow a team of guards to accompany you.' He sighs. 'All the good your family did for this country and still the masses complain.'

Ma understands the people's anger. It has to do with failed promises and a certain deficit in public funds. There are gold coins and dollar bills languishing in a vault in Switzerland. She has not used them, but her hands are tainted. She is a woman on the run. Not a woman going on vacation.

The Minister is telling her that.

'Only one guard. And I will interview him,' she says.

The Minister sends her a list of names, all top soldiers from the elite Presidential regiment. She rejects them one by one. They could not save her husband. What use will they be to her?

'These boys are like preening peacocks. I want someone quiet and fleet-footed like a deer. I should not even see him. A wisp of smoke: is what I want,' she tells the Minister.

The Minister listens, increasingly desperate. The woman

is disposable; it's her family name he has to protect. 'Ma—' he begins.

She cuts him short. 'If you can't find me such a man, I'll travel alone with my pistol.'

The Minister's wife suggests a name one night over dinner.

His scowl becomes a smile. The retired police officer was perfect. Sparrow small and alert with quick run around eyes.

'I have found your man,' he tells Ma the next day.

∞

The hotel sprawls behind the shoulder of a low brown hill. Ma has chosen it for its anonymity and ragged air. The air conditioning doesn't quite work and the bar only stocks local liquor. It's January so the place is quiet, except for a few retired couples doing crossword puzzles.

The first week she takes her breakfast in the main restaurant. Waiters flutter around her like flies. She dismisses them all. She sits alone in an alcove, the pistol in her lap like a sleeping dog. Large tortoiseshell sunglasses hide her eyes as she examines the other guests, couples no older than her, buttering their toast in silence. Boredom thrashing its wings between them. How different to when she sat with her husband in their garden, their skin still thrumming to the other's touch. His absent-minded fingers reaching out to caress her chin.

'Happy, my love?' That was his first and last question to her each day. 'Happy enough,' she always answered, even if

79

her heart somersaulted in fright as she began to adapt to the ways of her new life. She learnt quickly. He was proud of that. 'My love, in one year you speak the language of power better than me. If something happens to me, I know the country will be safe in your hands.' She'd pressed her thumb against his mouth. She wanted a simple life, two kids, a dog, a rose bush in the front garden. Instead, here she was – the wife of a leader who ruled over a billion people. He always laughed away her fears. 'Don't worry. No one dare touch me. I am the head of state. Invincible,' he'd said pulling her towards him, his face buried in the nape of her neck, pressing her closer to him until all she could hear was the urgent hoof-beat of his heart.

The first attempt at murder was clumsy. An arrow arced through the open window and landed at their feet as they sat eating dinner. Her husband shook his head sadly while she trembled with fear. 'We should leave this country.' She implored him every day. He refused, folding her inside the crook of his arm. 'This is our destiny. We're here to serve our country.'

Ma pushes away her breakfast.

To be left in peace. To walk barefoot beneath an unblinking blue sky and the babble of birds cracking open the day's light. She wades into the sea, the shock of the water making her toes curl in fright and then delight. It is back to her long-ago childhood. Her father holding her hand, coaxing her into the waves, his arms strong around her tiny waist.

She shoos away the memory. What matters is the now. The waves humming their song and the shuffling of the diminutive man who follows her, five paces behind.

Munshi. Her bodyguard. The one she chose. There he stands, quivering chin and clammy hands. She has that effect on people. He bowed and touched her feet when he first met her.

'I will protect you until my dying day.' His breathless promise. Yet one puff of air and the man would collapse, all rattling limbs and shrunken skin.

'Munshi may not look strong but he is wily like a snake and devoted like a dog,' the Minister had assured her, and she chose to believe him.

It could all be 'tamasha' for all she knew. Her husband's word for those who play-acted their sorrow and love.

'We are a nation of tamasha players,' he told her on that final day, before leaving to meet his death, greeting the adoring fans baying for him at the gates and the waif of a girl who had ducked through the crowds and aimed her dynamite straight at his heart.

She had let down her husband on his last day. Crowds bored her, so she'd told him to go out alone and bask in their applause. She was sitting at her dressing table, massaging her scalp with oil that smelled of Alpine pine needles when she heard the police sirens shrill, the cawing of crows, the bleating of the ambulance horn, the wailing of the Party faithful bereft of their leader.

'Shush!' She had shouted. Was it too much to ask for

silence?

He lay at her feet, a heap of broken bones and charred flesh. Vultures circled his smashed head and nowhere for her to run. Overnight she turned from a young wife to Ma, the nation's mother, the slain leader's widow, swapping her silks and pearls for threadbare home-grown cotton. It was what her husband would have wanted.

∞

She sits on a deck chair and waits while Munshi bargains for coconuts from the hawkers on the beach. 'Nectar of the Gods,' he says, presenting it to her. He has soft hands. She notices them as he cuts a precise cross into the mouth of the coconut shell. He arranges the slices like flower petals on the paper plate.

No one disturbs her on these walks. A straw hat hides her face. The sari-draped Ma smiling from the billboards and the woman walking on the beach are not the same. She gives Munshi time off for lunch. She knows he likes to frequent the nearby village where fishermen shacks double up as luncheon places.

Politely, she enquires about his meal. Food is important in a poor country. She discovered that as a shy twenty-year-old bride. 'Why is there so much discussion about eating?' She asked her husband. He cupped her face gently between his hands and said, 'My love. You now belong to a country where the scarcity of food makes it sacred. Every grain of rice is a gift of God. Don't ever mock it.'

'Jackfruit curry, fried prawns with ginger and lemon rice,' Munshi recites each dish like a poem. 'How about you, Ma? Did you get room service?' She changes the topic. She is giving up on food. At night, standing before the bathroom mirror, she counts her ribs. The gentle dip and swell of them. Blue veins spring over her body, like tributaries of a river searching for their source. With her index finger, she traces the outline of her sagging breasts. Her eyes are beginning to film over with a mucus cloud. She takes to wearing sunglasses even indoors.

A week after their arrival at the hotel, Munshi drags a camp bed into her room. There have been rumours about students from a nearby university planning an attack.

'For security purposes', he assures her. 'You see Ma, any unscrupulous cad can come and wreak havoc. Nowhere is safe.'

'They won't get much from me, Munshi,' she replies, adjusting the glasses on the ridge of her nose. 'But suit yourself. I will be lost in my dreams.'

She narrows her eyes and examines him.

'Do you have a family?'

Munshi shrugs and fidgets with his shirtsleeves. He swallows twice before speaking.

'My mother died last year. No Mrs or children. It's only me keeping me company in my old age.' He grins but it is an admission of defeat.

Ma pats his arm. They are both equally alone, she thinks.

∞

At night, pillow tight against his cheek, Munshi hears her sob. The murmur of words in a language he can't understand. Munshi knows that Ma has come from distant lands, planted her roots and made this country her home, but in the deep womb of night, she still calls out to the Gods in her mother tongue.

Ma begins losing weight. Her cotton tunics flap around her body.

Munshi offers her slices of pizza or soft squidgy cheese to remind her of her homeland. She shakes her head and refuses. He reports his findings to the Minister.

'Make sure Ma eats and hide her pistol. We don't want her making a martyr of herself. It will destroy the Party's image,' the Minister instructs.

Munshi goes through her things while she is in the shower and finds the pistol wrapped in a muslin scarf underneath her copy of the King James' Bible and a foreign chequebook.

She doesn't even notice it gone.

Ma wants to be by the sea but is too frail now to walk the long rust expanse of the beach.

Munshi procures a wheelchair from the local hospital and away they go, rubber wheels grunting through the sand, frightening away the murmuration of starlings swooping over the water. He pushes her to her favourite spot where the blue-grey waters of the Mandavi River merge into the teal green of the sea.

84

He retreats sitting on his haunches, eyes alert to danger, springing up to adjust the pashmina around Ma's sloping shoulders when the breeze displaces it. Is he in love with her? Maybe a little. He craves the simplicity of the early days when she took over the Party leadership from her dead husband. The trains ran on time and the 8 pm curfew meant all the troublemakers were tucked up in bed every night.

Strange forces are at play in his country now. Football stadiums and call centres burst like shooting stars out of nowhere while farmers swallow pesticide and commit suicide. In the cities, the hungry folk prowl, looting empty shops, their bellies distended with hunger. The new leader forms committees and panels. They draw algorithms on laptops and call Chinese IT experts. But nothing seems to get better. Every fortnight, cargo planes loaded with the rich and their briefcases crammed with money, silently take off in the thick of night to friendlier pastures across the seven seas. By God, she must be bitter, her country has failed, he says to the Minister. Her eyes water, her mouth droops.

Only once does Munshi pluck up the courage to question her.

'Ma. Do you want to be in power again?'

'Power?' she spits out the word. 'For what?' She extends her hands like a beggar woman.

'My only child lives thousands of miles away. My husband is dead, murdered by his own countrymen. Everywhere I look, I see daggers and fake smiles. Power again? No thank you.'

The years of brutality and civil war. She remembers them at night. The orders she signed. The knock on the door of those who opposed her. 'One must rule with an iron fist,' her husband always told her. 'Any sign of softness, and you'll be crushed like an ant. The people are poor. They don't know what is good for them. We must lead them.' She had done just that after his death. The Party pushed her to the top and she had followed his instructions like a prayer, sparing no one, not even her own nephew snatched away one morning. His face was damp with sweat, as he stood on the front step of his house with pyjamas soaked with his urine. They had never heard from the boy again.

∞

Ma sighs. The sea must wash away so much. Munshi helps her stand. She lets the sea run over her feet, wading deeper until it reaches her waist. Her damp tunic clings to her, the shape of her breasts and thighs clearly visible. Munshi lowers his eyes.

'Don't go deeper, Ma, please,' he pleads from the edge. 'I can't save you. I don't know how to swim.'

'I'm pure now,' she shouts. Her arms stretch wide open. Things float up to her. Offerings from the sea that she shares with Munshi. A dead starfish sleeps within the pink of her palm. Objects swirl around her: a dolphin's fin, clumps of withered coir, jerry cans discarded by trawler ships. A cracked child's rattle. Scooping it up from the water, she presses it to her chest.

'Let's go back, Munshi. I've no wish to see dead things.'

The evenings are long in the hotel by the sea. Most guests retire to their rooms or drink the local rum sitting on their porch, their eyes liquid with loneliness in the dying light. Munshi and Ma play cards in the billiard room that has no billiard table. Portraits of her dead husband line the walls but Ma does not glance at them, she is intent on winning her hand. Occasionally she lets Munshi win and they celebrate with a cup of cardamom tea. He takes her by the elbow and they walk back slowly to her room. All shame is gone, she lets him undress her and sponge her tired body with a cold towel. He massages her scalp and sings her folk songs from his village in the mountains.

She wants stories to help her sleep. Simple tales of kings and queens. 'Let the good destroy the evil,' she whispers, her voice small and hoarse. The story she loves the most is the one about the young doe-eyed girl who falls in love with a prince and changes the map of her life.

'Again,' she implores when Munshi reaches the story's end. She corrects him. 'No, we didn't meet in the library. It was a teashop. I accidentally dropped tea on his white linen shirt. His eyes twinkled when I offered to cook him chicken with olives and garlic.' She laughs. 'I was a good cook in my day.' She pauses, takes off her glasses, and rubs them with the hem of her tunic.

Munshi feels his heart squeeze tight when he hears this.

The Minister of Home Security calls Munshi daily,

precisely at 3 pm in the afternoon.

'Make sure she eats. Talk about the old times. Keep Ma alive. She is a symbol of our golden past.' There is a pause. 'Or else there'll be trouble.'

The new whip-smart leader is no longer to the country's taste. The people want Ma back. They have forgotten the disappeared or the dollars sleeping in the bank vaults.

One day, the Chief Minister arrives at the hotel along with a team of doctors.

'Ma. It is decided. We'll put you forward as our candidate at the next election. The Party needs you. This is not the time to hide. You can go back to being the nation's leader You're back in fashion.' The Minister's mouth smiles but his eyes are watchful.

Ma offers him tea and cashew biscuits. 'Cashews are a speciality of the region,' she explains. The fleet of doctors hover over her, syringes and stethoscopes ready. She shoos them away like flies and claps her hands.

'Away with you all. I only need Munshi.'

She is smiling the next morning.

'I think I'll eat today. I've a craving for croissants and cappuccino.'

Munshi takes this as a sign of new beginnings.

Just before their walk to the beach, she asks for her pistol.

He hesitates, folds his arms behind his back. Shakes his head.

She holds out her hand.

'Munshi. We have an understanding. Do we not?'

He weeps, kneeling down, huddled at her feet like a child. She pats his head.

'You're a good man. I need you to protect me.'

He understands her. He sees the arc of her remaining days filled with the frenzy of winning votes. The Party's sharp elbows pushing her forward. Not letting her trip. Or fall. Or fail. She was old. She deserved better.

He hands her the pistol.

There are instructions he must follow. She tells him about the envelope under her pillow.

'There is a cheque for your troubles and a one-way ticket to America.'

Ma's voice trembles. She removes her sunglasses. Her pink-rimmed eyes, crusted with mucus stare into his, unwavering and direct.

'It's best you start a new life. The Party won't forgive you for letting Ma go. Not with elections around the corner. They will want your blood.'

He wheels her to the water's edge. The sea is calm. A flock of seagulls swoops over her head.

'They are crowning you, Ma,' Munshi says.

He touches her feet to receive her blessing one last time.

She speaks quickly. 'Go back to the room and pack your bags. Your new passport will be at the check-in counter at the airport. When you reach New York, call this person.' She fumbles in her pocket and brings out a creased envelope.

He recognises the name. It is her son.

'Tell him, I forgive him,' she says.

She hands him her pistol like a bouquet of flowers and kneels down at his feet, bowing her head as though in prayer.

The pistol feels heavy in his hand. He shifts it from one hand to the other.

'I command you.' Her voice is gruff as she raises her face to look at him one last time. He notices the soft down covering her cheeks. She looks almost girlish in the early light.

The gunshot rings out, cracking the stillness of the day.

Soul Sisters

Suman Bakshi rents a room on a quiet street in West Didsbury. She has grey eyes. She works as a filing clerk at the Platt textile museum, a rundown red brick converted mill that squats on the outskirts of the city, just beyond the roar of the M56 motorway. The work is slow. Few people can be bothered to climb down the twenty steps to her basement office where she keeps the records on Eighteenth century spinning and weaving practises. She has plenty of time to read her novels, file her nails, or tweeze out stray eyebrow hairs in a small magnifying mirror she hides in her desk drawer.

But on this particular day Suman has been busy fielding queries from an American researcher who wants to know about the impact of imported Indian cotton on Lancashire mills. 'Well, there was Gandhi's boycott of British clothing...' she hesitates. Her knowledge of Indian history is threadbare. She blames her mother for the gaps in her knowledge, for insisting that the best way of assimilating in England was to memorise the names of Henry VIII's beheaded wives rather than know about Gandhi's Dandi salt march for India's Independence.

Nipping out for a sandwich at lunch, Suman spots a man hunched over an ATM in the corner. She knows it is Ashok. He has the same stooping shoulders and dark hair that turns henna red when the sun hits it. She quite liked the chameleon colour change, said it made him look like a Bollywood hero. The man, his back still to her, stuffs the money in his back pocket and walks rapidly down a side street towards the railway station. She keeps up with him as far as she can, until he disappears down a set of steps. But it's not Ashok. How can it be? He has moved down south, to Cheltenham with a new woman, an Englishwoman who now shares his life and watches him snore night after night.

She leaves work earlier than usual, hurries home, changes into her blue velour track suit with its faded bleached back pocket and her fluffy Disney slippers. Cuddling a bowl of Maggi chicken curry noodles, she slumps on the sofa with a book. It is Suman's third reading of Narshida Malik's novel, *The Nightingale of Kansas*. The bruised cover shows a blindfolded bird inside a cage. A few pages are folded into little origami fans with entire passages highlighted in yellow. The scribbled comments and underlined passages are the milestones by which she navigates her life. 'Unfeeling brutes,' she writes on page fifty-five, straight after this:

'The boys came up to me as I waited in the queue at Macdonald's. 'Aren't you boiling in this Mrs Osama Bin Laden? What are you-a letterbox? How will you post the burger? They shouted as I pushed past them and ran home, their spit hanging on my niqab. They made me feel ashamed to be me.' (pg. 55, *The Nightingale of Kansas*)

Suman underlines the last line and stops reading.

She closes her eyes, sinks back on the bed, the book nestling between her breasts and remembers. It was a warm

July. A Saturday. The heat was like a razor blade slicing her skin. She was at the Arndale centre, window shopping. Hot and sticky, she'd bought herself an ice-cream cone. Peanut brittle and Vanilla. A gaggle of school boys, satchels slapping against their thighs, snorted as they walked past her. 'Percy Piiiig...' Their voices still ring in her ear. At forty two, she is still surprised by the careless cruelty of the human male.

Suman sighs, gets up and walks to the fridge. She is hungry again. There is a Tupperware container with leftover chana and rice. She eats it cold, her back pressed against the thrumming front of the fridge. The spoon diving in and out of the container until it is empty. She thinks about calling her mother, telling her about how she'd almost seen Ashok and lost him. But she decides against it.

'Wake up, Suman. Stop day dreaming and hiding in them bloody books,' Is what her mother would say.

∞

Ashok had walked out on her fortieth birthday, leaving her stranded at the George and Dragon, alone with her half-finished lemonade. It was the royal wedding and their local was strung up with red and blue union jacks and men spilling on to the pavements gripping pints of lager. Women stood together, mouths knit in cautious dreamy smiles. The pub had put up a giant screen in the car park and there was much oohing over the bridesmaid's backside. Suman had felt quietly proud standing in the car park, staring at the confetti on the screen, proud to be sharing her birthday with royalty.

Ashok had told her to come inside.

'We'll miss the wedding vows,' she complained as she followed him. All the tables were empty, but Ashok led her to the farthest one, the one near the Ladies. Stupidly she had thought he was going to give her a surprise gift. He knew she had her eyes on an Omega watch.

'The thing is, Suman,' Ashok said. 'I don't think I'm in love with you anymore.'

His hands lay flat on the oak table, and he was studying his fingers as though they were arrows telling him which way to run.

A roar came from outside and Suman wasn't sure if the crowd was cheering Ashok or Prince William.

She spent the rest of the afternoon sitting on the toilet, her head in her hands.

He had found someone else. It was as simple as that.

∞

The room is dark. Suman switches on the television. She needs the noise and the flicker of light. The news is on. Another bomb explosion in Kabul or maybe it is Baghdad, she can't be sure. She stares at the images. It is like a video game, the streaks of light shooting against the dark of the sky. She hopes Narshida is okay, even though she knows Narshida lives in America, but one can never tell with writers. Their research can lead them anywhere. Especially a woman like Narshida – at times Suman feels that every word she reads is written with a pen dipped in blood.

Narshida's photo is taped on her wardrobe mirror. She'd found the photograph in an out of date issue of Time magazine at the dentist's. The picture reveals a woman with troubled eyes. Her mouth is full and dark. Suman imagines it painted a crimson red. She walks up to the photo and strokes the deep lines running down the sides of the mouth. She has similar lines. She runs a thumb down the sides of her nose. There they are, like a railway track.

'Do something Suman, slap on some foundation, some lipstick,' her mother said after Ashok's exit. 'You've got to look young to find another man.'

And Suman did try. She went to Debenhams, pulled out Narshida's picture from her bag and told the gum-chewing girl at the makeup counter. 'Make me like her.' But she came back home the same.

∞

It began quietly, the love affair with Narshida Malik. Suman had visited the local library one afternoon, her winter coat hiding her fleecy pyjamas. She stood bewildered in front of a shelf of books until the librarian, Mrs Jones came up to her and placing a hand on her shoulder, asked if she needed help.

'Do you have any instruction manuals on how to be happy? Some sort of do it yourself guide?' Suman did her best to force back the tears, gulped hard and told herself she wasn't going to cry.

'Why would you need such a book, my dear?' Mrs Jones voice reminded Suman of black and white films.

'We're not engines that need fixing,' the woman continued. And Suman's eyes had welled up at such unexpected kindness.

Mrs Jones handed her a box of tissues.

'But then again, I may have just the book for you. You will adore *The Red Rose of Kabul* by Narshida Malik. She is a foreigner like you, but she is very clever. Every word is written in English and it falls like a tear drop,' Mrs Jones said, walking briskly to the shelf at the farthest corner of the library.

'What is it about?' Suman asked politely, her eyes scanning the shelves for a book with a bold, chirpy cover, something like *How to Win friends and Influence People*.

'It's about a woman whose husband abandons her and goes off to war,' Mrs Jones said, her eyes glinting inside her red framed spectacles. 'That's men for you...forever chasing skirts and glory,' she added, handing Suman the book like a gift.

Suman wondered if Ashok was seeking glory and not a skirt when he walked out on her.

She read the novel in one sitting, rooting every step of the way for Noor, the proud protagonist who defied tradition.

'Life did not have to end just because your man walked out the door, the seasons still changed; she still had a brain and a healthy body.' (pg. 70, *The Red Rose of Kabul*)

She copied out the words in her notebook. And once finished, went back for some more. In six months, Suman had read the library's entire collection of Narshida Rashid's books.

She writes to Narshida's publisher in New York. The letters come back unanswered.

Suman files them carefully in chronological order.

'It won't be long before Narshida visits England. I can feel it in my bones,' she confides in Mrs Jones. The two women have become close. Not friends exactly, but they sometimes share a coffee at the Costa on Wednesdays when the library is closed.

'I'm sure I heard something about a book tour on Radio Four, but I could be mistaken,' Mrs Jones replies and passes her, *The Tears for the Unknown*.

'Keep up with your reading and stay well clear of men. They ought to come with a health warning,' she says, squeezing Suman's arm.

∞

A month later, she receives a telephone call. It's her brother.

'How's life, Suman?' He asks his voice Cola Light. He doesn't really care. She knows that. They are siblings, but their planets spin on different axis. And on her part she doesn't begrudge him his tinsel-happy life as a young man earning good money in the city.

'The usual stuff, Jai' she replies and waits.

'Are you sure you've not got your head buried in one of

them…Arab woman's books?'

She can hear his snigger down the telephone line.

'Narshida is of Afghan heritage, not Arab. She spells out the distinction carefully.

'Well, guess which Arab chick is coming to town,' Jai says.

∞

Suman rings in sick the next day and spends the day hunting for a new dress. She settles on a silk dress with a scarlet and black roses print. On her way home, she stops by the library and shows the dress to Mrs Jones, lifting it out of its tissue wrapping like a magician pulling a rabbit out of a hat.

'Fit for a bride, not that you'd want to be repeating that mistake again, my dear,' Mrs Jones says. 'I bet it cost a fortune.'

'I wanted the best,' Suman replies. 'How else will Narshida know it's me?'

She is travelling to London to meet Narshida who is on a whistle-stop tour to launch her new book.

Suman reaches Euston and calls her brother. He can't meet her, 'Important stuff at the office. Some of us have to work for a living you know.'

She imagines him at his desk: shoulders tense, face pushed against a computer screen.

'Your ticket for the reading will be waiting at the box office,' he says.

The rest of her day is a blur. She has a vague memory of crowds rushing past, the orange marmalade of the sun spread thinly across the sky. At some point she must have been hungry, she remembers the mushroom pizza at the Pizza Hut by Trafalgar square, the Cath Kidston tote crammed full of books digging into her hip.

She is early for the book launch. She orders a bottle of Shiraz, and a packet of crisps. She opens her notebook and begins to write.

Question one for Narshida: 'Can I persuade you to hold a reading in Manchester? There is a lovely old lady from the local library. She is a fan too. Maybe I will even cook for you. My ex-husband Ashok loved my cooking.'

Question two...

When she looks up, the bottle is empty and there is a queue outside the auditorium.

'Excuse me, excuse me...yes, family... friend of the author... special reserved seat... special needs,' she shouts, pushing past people, breathless by the time she gets to her seat.

Jai hasn't got her a front row ticket. But at least she has a clear, unrestricted view of the stage.

'Narshida's late. Isn't she? But then she is the star of the show.' She turns companionably to her neighbour, a bespectacled girl who scowls and mutters something inaudible.

∞

Lights dim. Silence falls. A short haired woman comes on stage and takes the microphone. Suman wants the crowd to stop snivelling and shuffling and scratching. The woman

99

taps on the mic to make sure it's working. A crackle echoes throughout the room.

'Ladies and gentlemen welcome to an evening with Narshida Malik….' She clears her throat and explains that Narshida is in the middle of a global world tour launching her new book. Angelina Jolie has already snapped up the film rights.

Suman edges forward in her seat, her knees squashed together.

'That's my girl,' she whispers. Her chest swells in pride.

The crimson velvet curtains part and there she is, standing before her. Just for her. Narshida's head is covered with a brown silk scarf and a turquoise necklace shines across her chest. The crowd starts clapping but Suman stays silent. Her hands are shaking as she lifts her camera and stands up. Murmurs of disapproval rise around her.

Narshida stares at her, framed in her lens, her black hooded eyes – still and mysterious. The interviewer stands up from her chair and grabs the mic.

'Please, no photographs. Narshida doesn't like the flash.'

The interview begins. Suman leans forward, tilts her head so she can listen clearly. She hears an American voice as Narshida reads aloud, flicking through the pages of her new novel, *The Nightmare of Baghdad*.

'I won't let you go out without wearing the hijab. What will the world say? Nadia shook her head. You are my brother, not my protector. I will dress and live how I want…'

A woman starts clapping. Narshida raises a hand to silence her and continues. Suman is listening but the words spin inside her head.

Looking around she sees rapt hands move across paper jotting down phrases. She too should be noting down Narshida's words, instead, she is sweating and fidgeting. She blames the two hour train journey and the wine.

The reading finishes. Narshida closes her book and turns to the interviewer.

'I won't be taking any personal questions, so please don't ask me about my dog, my lover or the kind of flowers I like to smell.'

The crowd titters. Suman's hand shoots up. The boy with the roving mic walks towards her. His purple tee shirt says he is against dolphin fishing.

The insides of Suman's thighs stick together, damp with sweat. Her breath is sour. The moment to shine has arrived. She knows her question: 'Narshida, are you happy? Do you ever get homesick for love?'

But Narshida's American voice, her elegant clothes and the way she drapes herself over her chair makes her question sound foolish.

'Do you have a question?' The interviewer frowns. The mic hovers over Suman's face like a missile. She opens her mouth and sneezes.

Suman sits down, head bowed, listening to the others. There are questions about Narshida's writing. A man shyly admits he's doing his PhD research on her. Narshida nods and lifts her hand to cover a yawn.

∞

It is over. People rush outside to form an orderly queue for the signing. Suman takes her place, her tote unzipped, full of books waiting to be signed. It is clear to her that she needs to be alone with Narshida. Only then can they reveal their true vulnerable selves to each other.

The organiser hands out post it notes for the crowd to write out their names.

'Only one name, one book, no personal messages,' she announces. 'Narshida has a BBC interview right after. Please don't delay her.'

Suman writes her name and scribbles, 'Please meet me for a coffee, Narshida. We have so much pain in common. We are soul sisters.'

It takes her forty-five minutes to reach the table where Narshida sits, pen poised.

Suman places the novels in front of Narshida like corpses awaiting resurrection. Narshida signs one, pushes away the rest, including the note. Suman leans forward.

'I want you to read my message. Read it now please.'

Narshida gives her a quick look and frowns.

'I don't have time. Can you see the queue?' She looks beyond Suman's shoulder.

'Next please.'

'There is no next please. You have to promise to meet me. We have a lot of catching up to do,' Suman pleads, still leaning on the table. Her bulk hides Narshida from the others. She must have raised her voice because the short haired woman who seems to be the organiser is moving towards her.

'What is the problem?'

Suman smiles. She finds it funny, all this fuss over a simple message.

'I just want my sister to read my note,' she says. 'That's all. She knows me well.'

Narshida starts laughing. Her teeth crowding her mouth are small and uneven.

'What sisters... Do I even fucking know you?' She picks up Suman's note and tears it up.

Tiny pieces scatter on the table like snowdrift.

'Will you please move away madam? Otherwise I will have to call security.' The organiser's hand is on Suman's shoulder, nudging her out of the way.

∞

The hall empties, but Suman waits by the door for Narshida to finish her BBC interview. A cleaner arrives, driving a little motorized hoover. Suman blocks his way, forcing him to stop.

'Are you all right, lady?'

'It's nice being called a lady,' she says. 'I just wanted to tell you that Narshida didn't mean to be rude. She was just jetlagged and tired, that's all.'

The cleaner looks confused so Suman waves him off.

She checks her watch. She's missed the last train home.

She sees Narshida, hurrying out of a side door, head bowed, deep in conversation with another woman. They walk quickly towards the exit. Suman follows them. Couples walk past, heads lowered, hands entwined, the click of their heels like a wedding march.

A thousand stars scar the sky.

A road appears. The woman beside Narshida hails a cab. They shake hands and she disappears. Narshida is alone. She crosses the road, lifting a hand to halt the cars and the buses. She has removed her headscarf and Suman sees that her hair is long and dark. She would like to run her fingers through her hair. Maybe Narshida will gift her a lock, a little memento of their meeting. The hair will carry her scent. Suman stops, she feels light headed. Her mobile rings. It's her brother. She lets it ring out.

Narshida is still walking and Suman steps up her pace, breathless by the time she catches up with her. But not quite. Narshida is still quicker. She enters a glass building with revolving doors. Suman looks up to read the sign. All that grand talk about a movie deal and she is only staying in a three star Mercure hotel. She would have to tell Mrs Jones about it. Why, if she had her way, she'd have booked Narshida a suite at the Ritz.

Suman walks into the hotel lobby, head bowed, rummaging through her bag, as though looking for a room key. A group of American tourists are at the check in desk, clutching maps and iPads. She sidles up behind them, waiting her turn.

'I am here to meet Miss Narshida Malik... an interview. I'm from the Museum of...' She flashes her staff card at the receptionist who is jabbing the computer in front of him, while answering the phone. He is young with a freckled face and a badge that says, 'Training.'

'Room 435.' He doesn't even look at her.

A Japanese couple are waiting for the lift. The girl, pale and slim, dressed in jeans and a tee shirt with little teddy bears embroidered in rhinestone.

'I like your tee shirt. It's cute,' Suman tells the girl once they are inside the lift. The couple bow together, their heads almost touching.

'You must be on your honeymoon. You like London?'

But she doesn't wait for their answer because the doors open, her floor is there.

∞

The night turns dark. The streets empty of people. A cyclist in a high visibility yellow jacket cycles past the short overweight woman walking towards the river.

She meant no harm. If only the stupid girl hadn't tried to shout. If only she had sat quietly on the bed and listened to her story. But no, Narshida had to act funny. Why couldn't she stop screaming? The only way to keep her quiet was to put the pillow to her face. There was stillness then. And Suman could finally tell her about Ashok. And smoke her cigarette. And tell her how much she loved her books.

Suman leans on the railing, watching the river, sleek and shiny with night time lights.

The bag with the unsigned books cuts into her shoulder.

She opens her bag and lets the books slip out into the waters below. They fall quietly, without making the slightest splash.

A Simple Man

My sister calls me from Birmingham. Out of the blue. We haven't spoken for months and here she is at the end of the phone.

'Pikku, I am coming to London to stay with you. I have problems at home.'

Her voice quivers like a bird caught on a barbed wire fence.

She pauses before continuing. 'Are you able you look after me?'

I know what she's asking. Can I support her? What could I say? She's my younger sister and she needs me.

'Of course, Bubbly,' I reply. 'Come and stay for as long as you want. I have a good job and I make enough.'

She lets out a long sigh of relief. 'Thank God for that. I know London is a costly city and I was worried that you wouldn't have a proper job that paid well.'

I knew what she meant by 'proper.' A job like my father's, sitting in a big office with important files on the desk and a secretary busy taking notes.

'I have a proper job,' I said, warily.

'I knew you would land on your feet one day. I am so proud of you,' she said, as though I am a goose that has finally laid a golden egg.

∞

Bubbly has been here for several days. I'm trying to distract her from her constant requests to visit me at work. It's a game that's becoming tedious and worrying.

'I would love to look around your office,' she says again, like a child clamouring to visit a toyshop. She calls it that even though I've explained that I work in a museum and although I have responsibilities, my duties aren't strictly professional. One day, someday soon, I will have to tell her the truth about my modest job that can barely pay the bills but for now I'm enjoying basking in the glow of her admiration.

On Sunday, she declares it's the perfect day for a visit. It is summer and it isn't raining. We would get off the tube at Waterloo, cross the metal bridge that bows beneath the weight of hurrying feet and begin our walk, strolling along the pavement that runs beside the river, not talking, but enjoying the sunshine warming our faces. Peace in our souls.

Wear something colourful for a change, I almost say, not your usual black sweatshirt and leggings but I don't want to disrespect her sorrow, the sorrow of a woman who has lost her husband. Bubbly is the baby of the family. When I look at her, I don't see a woman with greying hair and sloping shoulders who sucks in her cheeks when she is thinking hard. I see a plump-faced child in a lacy frock doing somersaults in our parents' garden in Kampala. The servants, Igbo, Homer, even old Mwamba the gardener are in a circle around her. They clap their hands and sway their heads, singing out her name as she flips over and over and rolls down the hill. The wind stirs the trees so that the white and pink flowers of the Coral tree fall over her head like a blessing.

Much has changed. Kampala is now just a name on a map. Today, Bubbly is a widow who has left her family home in Birmingham because she's fallen out with her son and his wife. It happens. One minute she is happily settled, the next minute she is on my doorstep, suitcase in hand. She has enrolled for an accountancy course through the Open University.

Bubbly is the clever one in the family. Me, I'm just a simple man. 'A dunce who will never amount to much. A simpleton,' my father snarled when I didn't get the grades to get into college in England. Even on his deathbed, he'd turned his head to Bubbly, gripped her fingers and promised her she would fly high. Bless your son too, my mother cried, pushing me towards his slowly dying face, but the light in his eyes dimmed and the doctor hushed us into silence.

Our afternoon walk soon brings us to the museum. There it stands, a concrete block that hugs the curve of the river's lip like a mole. The swollen white clouds floating above are mirrored in its shiny glass panes. Bubbly can't make up her mind whether it's beautiful or ugly.

'Maybe it's ugly in a beautiful way, bhaiya,' she says, eyes narrowed, her fingers drumming her chin.

I told you she is the smart one.

'It used to be a power station,' I explain. 'They want it to reflect its heritage, that's why it's so brutal looking.' I had stolen these lines from the visitors' pamphlets that lay like a pile of unwanted gifts at the museum entrance.

Bubbly nods her head, impressed. 'Now, let's see your room. I bet you have a big desk and an Apple computer.' Her voice rises in excitement.

'You think I have such a computer. And a big office?' I touch her hand and my eyes almost well up.

'Of course. Why wouldn't you, Pikku? Never underestimate yourself.' There she goes, shaking her finger like a schoolteacher.

I say it's too complicated to get us into the museum. She will have to get a pass, sign forms. 'Let's leave it for another day.'

She nods and pats my hand understandingly.

'Whenever you are ready,' she says, as we head back.

I am so lucky to have her as my sister. And the truth is I am ashamed. Ashamed to tell her I am just a humble guard who patrols the large rooms. I was lucky to get the job without any qualifications. I call myself the guardian angel of these paintings. Every day from nine to five, I stand at the door, watching the crowds shuffle past paintings, pause, shift, clear their throats, take furtive photos on their mobile phones until I walk across to them and warn them in a whisper loud enough for the room to hear, 'No flash please.' I press my index finger against my mouth and shake my head but always with a smile. I don't want to hurt their feelings.

I am too busy to notice the paintings, much like a

harassed mother with her brood of children, too busy head counting to notice the odd snivelling or tummy cramp. Instead, I stare at the visitors. They arrive, heads strapped to their audio guides, hands gripping phones, brochures, notebooks.

On Monday mornings, we get a briefing from the boss.

'Watch out for the rucksacks and the prams,' he shouts.

Single young men who linger too long before a particular painting, or whose hands dive into their pockets and spring out a camera are dangerous. I must walk over to them, my navy blue uniform announcing its authority, the walkie-talkie itching in my hand ready to leap into action. The boss comes close and jabs my shoulder with his thumb. 'You, you straw head. Are you listening? Don't start daydreaming about your Banglaland or wherever you come from, OK? Keep your eyes open.' His breath stinks of bacon. The other guards giggle and I laugh along with them. He means well. These paintings cost millions and I am their caretaker. My chest swells with pride.

Four years of service and I have seen them all. Rich, poor, the down at heel who use the museum to shelter from the cold and the lonely playing mating games within these walls. There are regulars who are almost friends. We exchange smiles and a wave. There's the mother who comes every Friday afternoon with her teenage daughter, apple cheeked and strong limbed. Arm in arm they stride from picture to picture, talking in excited whispers. It must be nice to have such a close mother daughter bond.

111

Then there is the Japanese gentleman who comes in a suit and tie, probably works in a bank. He carries a briefcase and a camera and pauses before each painting, looks in my direction, gives a slight bow of the head and takes the shot. I can't really shout at him because he's so gentle so I choose that moment to bend down and tie my shoelace or whisper a quick greeting to my colleague, Reginald, who is patrolling the next room.

'How is it going, bro?' I ask.

'I feel like a Pope in a brothel,' he replies, laughing.

Reginald is from Guyana but has Indian blood swimming somewhere deep inside him. For years, he's been pestering me to invite him home. 'Man, I want your curries, your roti meat,' he says, his voice wheedling with want. Maybe one of these days, I will bring him some of Bubbly's samosas but no way am I bringing him home to meet her. He has wandering eyes.

I wonder why people visit a museum. What do they want to see as they shuffle timidly past and stand respectfully in front of the paintings, eyes devouring the colour, squinting at the labels, looking for meaning. Is it something they can't find inside the arms of their loved ones or outside in the parks or in the temples and churches?

Once a week, Bubbly cooks my favourite childhood dish, luwombo with smoked chicken and plantain leaf. She shakes her head when I tell her how the people stand with open mouths in front of paintings of dead, pink and white kings and queens.

'Why should they rule us even after they are gone?' I ask her as I take second helpings of luwombo.

She says people are always looking for leaders to hold their hand, even if they end up with their hands chopped off. 'Just like Big Daddy Idi Amin.'

We say the name together and start giggling even though what he did to us was not very funny.

'I bet you're a good boss. A good leader to your team. I wish father was alive and he could see you,' she says, hugging my waist. I fall silent.

Sometimes the museum turns into a party place for the rich and the important. A quiet hush descends on the museum on such nights, the lights dim and smartly dressed young women arrive, their arms filled with red roses and trays of tea lights. There is the rustle of stiff white tablecloths swung over the trestle tables that are wheeled in for the occasion. I offer to help but the Polish men say they've got it all under control. Then the speeches begin. It's a pleasant drone that I don't even attempt to follow but some words stick out – 'abstract' is one and 'sensory impact' another. I will look them up in Bubbly's dictionary. My eyelids turn heavy as the voices carry on and to keep myself awake I try to spot the Indians. The men fiddle with their mobile phones and the women give me a glance and then look away, ashamed that one of their own is doing such a menial job. Once, an Indian lady had carelessly dropped her shawl. I scooped it up and gave it to her. 'Yeh lijiye…' I used my politest Hindi as I offered it to her but she was having none of it. Chin tilted in defiance and without so much as a thank you, she snatched it from me.

Reginald and I always volunteer to do double duty on such nights. It's an easy way to earn overtime, watch the wealthy as they eat and drink and exchange numbers. They spend most of the time admiring each other and not the paintings.

'Like bloody monkeys in a zoo,' Reginald whispers as he walks past me to take up his spot.

The girls glide around, holding titbits in decorative papier-mâché bowls. My stomach rumbles. How is it that the rich are never hungry? They peck at their food like peacocks.

These gatherings bring back the old days in Kampala when the autumn breeze had shooed away the last of the summer heat and the red dust on the roads had settled down. Father threw dinner parties for the VIPs or Very Important Parasites. That's what he called them in private. The house hummed with the sound of running feet and bustling hands, and mother shouting out orders to the servants in her thin reedy voice.

'Make sure you grate the ginger, not cut it in such thick slices. Is the mutton already cooked? Where is the lace table cloth?' Her voice travels across the lost years to find me on such evenings and I am grateful for the memory.

I would watch the ministers pull up in their long, sleek, white cars with flashing lights on the roof. Just as I was about to run to the gate to greet them, father's strong arms swooped me up.

'Where do you think you're going? Don't you dare come out and embarrass me, you dunce.' Bubbly welcomed the guests, reciting her nursery rhymes without forgetting a single word. The ministers patted her head and said she was a clever child.

∞

'There is a new exhibition opening in your office,' Bubbly says one day. 'They're having a major exhibition of an Indian painter. I read about it in the newspaper. He is called Atul Ghose?'

I feel my muscles tense when she says this. I'm supposed to know such things.

'Oh yes... of course.' Like a parrot, I repeat what I've heard the curator say. I may have a slow mind, but I also have quick ears.

Bubbly hugs me, her head with its thin, sparse hair pressed against my chest. 'My clever, clever brother. I am so proud of you,' she whispers, her quiet eyes smiling through her steel framed spectacles.

When I come back after the weekend, the walls of the museum are plastered with bold new posters. They show an Indian man with a goatee beard and sallow, aubergine-coloured smoker's lips. Atul Ghose, *The Enigma of Parting. Portraits of an Age*. That's what the posters say. I take out my little notebook and jot down enigma. One more word to add to my vocabulary. Seeing that Indian face with its brown

115

sunken cheeks and the inky shadows under the eyes makes me happy. I don't know why. It just does. My chest puffs out in pride when Reginald and I sit together in the canteen for lunch.

'Say Reginald, can you name me some painters from Guyana?' I ask him innocently.

He shakes his head. 'Nope cannot. This art business is a white man's game. Empty bellies have no time to paint.' His face looks momentarily sad and then clears up. 'It's all bullshit anyway, man.'

'We have painters in India,' I correct him. 'In fact if you care to look at the walls rather than scratching your balls, you will see one, Atul Ghose.'

'Is that so?' Reginald says. Eyes round like the moon. 'There are so many billions of you shits anyway; one of them was bound to end up with a paint brush.' He shrugs and turns to his egg-mayo sandwich.

The morning of the opening, I make sure my uniform jacket is finely pressed. The room is already buzzing by the time I arrive for my shift and take up my position. Clever types in black walk backwards and forwards, eyes screwed up into slits, punching furiously into their iPads and mobiles. The crowds finally thin in the late afternoon. It's been a bright day and sunlight leaks through the protective blinds of the museum windows brightening the room. I leave my post by the door and walk closer to the paintings. Let's see what this Atul Ghose is about.

The beauty stabs me right in the heart. Men and women crowd the canvas, colourfully dressed in Holi colours, deep in embrace. The night above them is sprinkled with a dusting of stars. Cows mew at their reflection in a pond flooded with lotus flowers. I read the title underneath the painting, *Krishna's love tryst with his Gopis.* Tryst, I jot in my book. I move to the next painting of a naked couple, arms entwined, sitting on a swing made of woven flowers. A dog prowls nearby, nibbling their toes. My face grows hot in embarrassment. Has the painter no shame? I look around, furtive. No one is watching, so I extend my finger and lightly brush it against the woman's exposed breast.

I find it difficult to sleep that night.

'It's that green tea you gave me,' I shout to Bubbly through my open door.

'Rubbish,' she snorts. 'It must be the beer you have been drinking with your colleagues.'

She means Reginald of course. Her bedroom is opposite mine, and we sleep, our single beds positioned so we can see each other's faces as we lie in bed, chatting until our eyelids grow heavy with sleep. I dream of elephants that night and of young bare-breasted girls dancing under a canopy of stars. When I wake up next day, the day is flat and grey like a dead fish.

Atul Ghose is a success. I turn up for work and there is already a queue snaking past the toilets, right up to the cafeteria. The crowds can't get enough of his blue-skinned Krishna and dancing ladies. Even the museum shop sells

117

out of fridge magnets and tea towels printed with Krishna's face.

'Well done on getting him,' Bubbly says that evening. She has been reading up on the exhibition. I wish she would focus on her accountancy papers, but no, she has to ask me a thousand questions about Atul Ghose. I tell her how he lives all alone on a farm in France.

'I would like to see his paintings,' Bubbly says.

'All the tickets are sold out.' I don't want her to see me in my guard's uniform.

Her mouth turns down and then reshapes into a smile.

'Don't worry about it, Pikku,' she says, tenderly. 'Maybe you can get me the catalogue.'

I look at her closely, trying to read her face like a map. How much does she know or not know? This would be the perfect time to tell her about my job. Tell her that I don't sit behind a big desk shouting orders. But, a voice inside me whispers, Don't tell her, she will be disappointed. Don't let her down. I decide to bring Atul Ghose home to her. I will borrow the painting of Krishna and Gopis show it to her and replace it. Simple. No more pestering, only pride in her brother. We will admire the painting together in the comfort of our home and she will explain the meaning of the fruits and the flowers in her clever, quiet way.

I wait and watch and one day when the day is ugly and sad with rain and the museum not that busy, I take my chance. At a certain point in the evening, the lights dim and the PA system coughs into life, urging the visitors to gather

118

their belongings and leave because the museum is about to shut. Footsteps start retreating like waves leaving the shore. There is silence. I walk up to the painting, pull out a pair of scissors from my pocket. My hands are shaking and I drop them. It feels wrong but then I see Bubbly's face. I can't go home empty handed. Snip. It is done. The painting falls into my arms like a baby. I tuck it under my armpit and begin the walk to the exit.

There is noise, a wailing whistle and flashing lights.

'What the fuck are you doing, man?' Reginald shouts as he spots me.

I begin running.

A Birthday Gift

Dad's tablets are scattered on the plate, a kaleidoscope of red, blue and green. Each pill is an arrow pointing to a tired liver, an erratic bladder, an unreliable heart. I hand him a glass of water and watch him gulp them down.

'You slept well, Dad?'

'Only three trips to the toilet.' He grins. The whites of his small eyes are freckled with pink veins and his rounded shoulders hunch forward as though ready for an embrace.

On this, his seventy-second birthday, he sits in my kitchen, wearing a maroon woollen scarf wound tight around his neck and a pair of white Nike trainers. The trainers are a last-minute purchase, bought at Delhi airport, just as he was about to board the England-bound plane in a pair of Bata flip-flops. The scarf and trainers are his armour against the British cold.

I bring Dad his toast and fried egg and a bowl of baked beans cooked the way he likes them, with chopped onions and roasted cumin. He eats slowly. His hand shakes as the fork reaches his waiting mouth and he pushes away the plate once he is finished. I wipe traces of the egg yolk from his chin with a tea towel.

'Happy birthday, Dad.' I bend down and lightly brush his bald head with my fingers. He smells of urine and dried sweat.

'Is that so? Is it my birthday, Sheila?' He looks round for

my mother.

She is on the sofa at the other end of the room, the newspaper spread open on her lap, a mug of tea nesting against her chin.

She nods. 'It's the same date every year. Why would it change?'

He smiles when he hears this.

'Thank you for remembering. Anita, my lovely beti.' He pats my arm.

'You're seventy-two, Dad. We need to celebrate. Isn't that so, Ma?' I turn to my mother, but she has her head down, reading the papers, her mouth soundlessly shaping the words.

'Let's go out for lunch. You love pizzas, Dad don't you?' I state this like a fact.

Ma looks up and frowns. She brings the tea mug closer to her mouth and shakes her head.

'Why bother. It will rain soon and he'll catch his death of cold.' Pulling her shawl tight around her shoulders, she walks to the window and stares at the rain-swollen heavy clouds drifting in the sky

I continue clearing the table.

'If we start waiting for the weather to clear up, we'll be stuck inside forever. It'll be a nice outing, Ma,' I say. 'It'll do you both good to get out. I'm taking the day off.' My voice is firm.

'Why make a fuss, beti? It is only an old man's birthday. Your Dad's hardly bothered.' Ma pauses and looks in his

121

direction.

Ma does not believe in celebrations. For my eighteenth birthday, she had gifted me a book, *The 7 Habits of Highly Effective People*. There was no party, no tinsel, no chocolate cake dizzy with candles to surprise me when I walked into the house. My mother is suspicious of happiness. Maybe it has to do with being a child of Partition. She was a schoolgirl in Lahore in 1947 when she came home from school one day, only to be rushed to a waiting train that sped her and her family to a new life across the border. Her toys and her friends all left behind. The fear of fleeing the familiar has never left her.

I hesitate. 'You might be right, Ma. We don't want Dad to catch a cold. It'll be nice and cosy at home. Why don't you cook your famous keema?'

Dad pushes back his chair noisily and stands up, glowering at us.

'I hate your keema peas, Sheila. You don't know how to cook,' he shouts, his voice trembling with effort. 'Let's go out and celebrate my birthday.'

I make soothing noises. I don't want his heart to give up on him. 'Hush now, Dad. Calm down.'

My parents are visiting after a long time. I imagine them leaving their bungalow one early morning, the sky alive with the cawing of crows, Ma counting the suitcases for the fifth time, Dad impatiently pointing to his watch and then waving goodbye to the servant standing at the gate with folded hands. It has taken them a week to recover from the ten-hour flight with its long stopover in Dubai, where the airport's fluorescent lights and potted plastic palm trees gave them both a headache.

'Dubai is like Disneyland for delinquent adults,' Ma grumbled when I picked them up at the airport. She sighed loudly and said she was too old for travel. All she wanted was to stay in bed for a week after the tiring journey.

I blame a long menopause for her crabbiness. Now that they are here, I want them to enjoy and I want to reassure them that despite living a continent away, I will still make time for them.

The rain clears by the time we reach the restaurant. Da Giovanni is the city's oldest, most authentic Italian, but it is practically empty that Tuesday afternoon. The vacant tables with their red and white checked tablecloths and small glass vases with a single pink carnation are like guests waiting for a party to begin. A middle-aged couple sit huddled in a corner, near the toilets. The woman plays with her hair, twisting it around her finger nervously.

Dad insists on keeping his overcoat on, though the restaurant is warm as toast and our table is next to the radiator. The waitress comes over to take our order. Ma wants vegetarian pizzas for all of us.

'No ham, no beef, but plenty of chillies,' she tells the girl who keeps saying, ya, ya. I imagine her to be Polish, or maybe Romanian. My cleaner has the same accent. Dad speaks to the waitress in Italian – broken phrases he has picked up somewhere along the way.

'Ciao, bella,' he mumbles. 'Ciao. Ciao.'

The girl leans forward to hear him better. The top three buttons of her green shirt are undone and I can see her lacy pink bra. She giggles and nods as she listens to my Dad.

Ma fiddles with the cutlery on the table, her eyes fixed on the waitress. Dad will not let me order champagne. Only coke. Just regular full-fat coke. Ma says it is bad for his diabetes.

'Drop it, Ma. One coke won't kill him,' I say glancing at my watch.

'What a slut. Did you see her bra?' she says after the waitress has left. I press her hand. 'Shh, not so loud. It's Dad's birthday.'

'Big deal,' she snarls and goes back to inspecting the menu. 'Look at these prices. Nearly six hundred rupees for a can of Coke.' She peers at me over her reading glasses.

'Are you sure you can afford this, Anita. You won't get into trouble, taking time off work?'

'Of course not. I can do what I want.' I roll up my sweater sleeves so my mother can see my Chopard watch with its twinkle of tiny dancing diamonds. I bought it on a whim in Geneva. The fact that I did not even ask for a discount made me feel smug and different to the other tourists who pressed their faces against the shop window but were too timid to enter.

Ma chooses to forget that I run my own law practice and live in a house with a paid mortgage. Because I am still unmarried at forty, it makes me fragile and needy in her eyes.

'A little knock and you'll break without a man's protective arms to cushion your fall.' She says this every time the talk comes round to settling down and finding Mr. Right.

Ma picks up her napkin, spreads it on her lap, sniffs it and then refolds it before placing it back on the table.

'You should see the restaurants in Delhi. So smart, so clean.'

I am too tired to contradict her.

The waitress reappears with our food. She insists on cutting up Dad's pizza.

'Nonno, sweet nonno,' she calls him, cutting a little piece, skewering it with the fork and holding it towards his open mouth.

'That's enough.' Ma grabs the fork from the girl's hand. 'He can feed himself, he's not a baby. Go back to the kitchen.'

Dad looks up from his pizza and says Ma is jealous of him. Jealous of the fuss the world is making over him. His eyes look puffy and small. White crumbs cling to the corner of his upper lip.

That evening he dozes in the study that I have converted into a temporary bedroom to save them the effort of climbing two flights of stairs.

Ma sits on the edge of the sofa in the kitchen, fidgeting with her hands. She has brought her bad mood back into the house.

I switch on the television, to her favourite Asian channel.

There is live reporting on a rape trial in Delhi. A twenty

125

year old girl was abducted on her way to college. The case has collapsed because the rapists have alibis.

I shudder. 'It is clear as daylight they're guilty. Look at them smirking. How can they get away with it?'

'Because they can,' Ma replies. 'They are men.' Her mouth sets into a thin line. She almost looks triumphant.

'I'm so glad I live in England. Life is much cleaner here, Ma, squeaky Dettol-clean,' I yawn. I have to be up early in the morning to place a call to Shanghai.

'Really? Are things that simple, Anita?' Ma asks. Her voice is flat. 'You think there's no violence against women here? What kind of a Mills and Boon lawyer are you?'

I feel my cheeks burn. How dare she call me a candyfloss lawyer cut off from reality?

'Of course stuff goes on here too, Ma, but it's not so raw, so ugly. Thank God, Dad isn't watching this. He is such a gentle soul. Do you remember when the neighbour's dog snuck into our house with a dead rabbit? He ran upstairs. He couldn't face it.'

'Yes, he's always been a coward.' The room is in shadows but I can feel Ma's eyes on me.

'What's got into you today? Leave Dad alone.' I stare at her, at her bird-like body folded inside her blue silk tunic and salwar.

Ma swallows and pinches the loose fold on her neck.

'There's something I've been meaning to tell you. I have waited a long time, but you never visit us and somehow these things can't be said on the phone.' The words stumble out in a rush and her hands fall back into her lap, clasped together as if in prayer.

The TV babbles on. I pick up the remote to turn down the volume, but Ma shakes her head. 'Keep it loud.' She tilts her chin towards the door. 'I don't want him to hear.'

'Your Dad's not what you think he is,' she says and reaches out to caress my cheek.

'He is fine, Ma. Dad is just fine.' My voice rises while inside me I shrink back to the small, shy girl who passed her childhood evenings watching her parents sit together in silence. Mother's hands busy with knitting, Dad's eyes fixed on his office files. The whirring noise of the ceiling fan, the only sound of the evening. I couldn't wait to escape.

'Your Dad's done wrong. A big wrong. And like those rapists on television he's got away with it.' Ma hesitates, checks my face to see if I am listening.

'I don't understand.' I frown and lean forward.

'Many years ago, when I was expecting you and I was in hospital for the delivery, your Dad made a girl pregnant.'

Her mouth fires out these words like small round bullets. I feel my stomach churn and the sour tomato taste of the pizza rises up my throat.

I imagine a one-night stand with an office secretary or a family friend who betrayed my mother's trust.

Ma hesitates and then mentions a name. 'Kusum,' the Nepalese maid my parents once employed. I had heard the name through the years, mostly in passing, when mother would fire a cleaner and say, she wasn't as thorough as or as honest as Kusum.

Kusum's name now comes up again and stands in front of us like an unwanted gift on my Dad's birthday.

'How could he make her pregnant?' I whisper, not wanting to believe. I edge closer to Ma and place my head on her bony shoulder, my cheek pressed against her neck where a faint pulse murmurs like Morse code. She is here with me, but she is also far away watching a dusty, grainy film from some place I don't recognise.

Ma is getting senile and she is imagining things. Old age does that to people, a lifetime of anger rising up like balloons and set free one after another. It is a kind of release.

'She was only sixteen,' Ma continues. 'A child really. I came back from the hospital with you in my arms, a tiny baby you were with your big bright eyes and she was at the door holding a garland of marigold flowers to welcome me back.'

She scowls at the memory. 'Anyway, Kusum started being sick soon after, turned pale like a bedsheet, throwing up in the kitchen and I thought she's caught a bug, probably ate some rubbish, some chaat or samosa in the market, so I took her to the doctor.'

Ma pauses and looks towards the door. We can hear Dad snoring.

'The doctor told me Kusum was pregnant. I dragged her home and gave her two hard slaps. We are a decent family. How dare you spoil our good name?' Ma turns to me, a ghost of a smile on her lips. 'Funny how I still remember the exact words I used. She burst into tears and told me everything.'

I move away and shake my head. I want to hit Ma for inventing such lies.

'Why would Dad do that? He's a good man.' My father has spent his life being a good man. At his retirement party, his colleagues presented him with a silver tray carved with his initials and the inscription, "There goes a good man." The tray holds pride of place on their mantelpiece at home.

Ma ignores me and carries on. 'He was abusing her for a year. He would come home for lunch, wait until I was having my afternoon nap and then order Kusum to follow him to the study. He always found some excuse, maybe to help him look for an old file. Stupid, stupid me. I could not see it.'

Ma's hands fold into fists and she starts striking her forehead. She does this quietly, without making a sound. I take hold of her hands and keep them locked in mine.

'Why didn't you call the police?' I feel I am eavesdropping on a stranger's crime.

'I confronted him. He smiled and denied it. Said the girl was blackmailing a good man, spoiling our family name.'

'And you chose to stay on?' I can barely look at Ma.

'I stayed on.' Ma repeats my words. 'What else could I do? I was young. I had you. My parents wouldn't have let me divorce. I chose to believe him even though there were other girls, always poor, always desperate for a job. He was careful after that. He paid them, took precautions. And he

129

was a good father. He was so proud when you became a lawyer in England.' Her voice falls.

I let go of her hands. Deep within my bones, a memory stirs. The soft knock on the door late at night. Dad entering my room to tuck me in, make sure I was asleep. His hands slipping under the bedsheet, warm on my skin. 'Count to ten and keep your eyes shut.' His hot murmur in my ear. The sound of trickling water as I scrubbed away the shame. Next day there was ice cream after school and a wink that said I was Dad's special girl. And suddenly I want my parents to pack up and leave, dragging their shameful little secrets behind them. I want my life back – uncluttered, unshaded, Dettol-clean.

The rain starts. The raindrops beat like drums against the windowpane. We sit in darkness, mother and daughter. There is a world outside. People laugh, walk, and eat. We are not part of them.

'What happened to her?' I whisper, but I don't really want to know. I want to curl up somewhere far away by myself and fall asleep.

'I sold my gold bangle and put her on the first bus to Kathmandu. She begged me to not send her away. She said she couldn't go back to her village with that dishonour growing inside her.'

'Let's find her.' I stand up, switch on the lights, and suddenly remember that I am an adult woman, a lawyer who can make wrong right. I look for my mobile phone. 'We can make up for lost time. Apologise.'

Ma throws me a pitying look.

'There's no need for that, Anita,' she says. 'She never reached the village. First thing she did when she got back to Kathmandu was put her head down on the railway track.'

Someone to Take My Place

Dr Kenan blinks at me through his blue framed plastic glasses.

'Cramps. It's nothing but cramps. Quite common. I can prescribe some blood tests but it might just be dysmenorrhea or menstrual pain,' he says in doctor speak. His mouth stinks of Polo mints.

The lying bastard. He has misdiagnosed and I know it. He holds up a CT scan of my stomach, pointing to a shadowy patch. 'All in your mind. See, nothing it's nothing, he'll say, blanking the shadow. But they are there. The cancer cells spread like a locust swarm. The image is beautiful like a Japanese charcoal drawing, all blurred shadows and silhouettes. My insides have mutated into a Haiku landscape.

So busy am I lost in this landscape, he has to clear his throat twice to make me sit up and notice him.

I curl my fingers one by one like a set of fishing hooks. 'Is that how long I have?'

He shakes his head vigorously, as though trying to get rid of dandruff. 'You are being unduly alarmed. We need further tests to make it conclusive. It could be a temporary inflammation.' I know what he is thinking. 'Hypochondriac and hysterical woman, but then she is foreign. They are used to hyper ventilating about most everything.'

Outside the summer afternoon light cuts me like a razor

blade. There is a café across the road where I order a cappuccino. The coffee with its trembling dust of chocolate heart grows cold as I rush to the bathroom, elbowing aside the young mum who is furiously trying to unstrap her bawling baby from the pushchair. I spend the next half hour in the bathroom, hunched over the toilet, doubled up with pain as my insides empty in a snowdrift of blood and mucus. There is no poetry in being ill anymore.

I am in this alone. Paul, my husband has only scorn for illness. He comes from the land of the able bodied and strong. 'You're exaggerating as usual, darling–' is what he says. Mind over matter and any other vanilla wisdom he can think of.

I decide to go on extended sick leave.

'It could be cancer.' I point to my tummy that sphinx like is hiding its secrets. He looks at me steadily, without blinking.

'You will be fine. The thing is not to give in.' He pauses and continues. 'I'm thinking of booking us a trip to Easter Islands. The statues are quite unique,' he announces in his persuasive BBC World Service voice. I smell his Hugo Boss aftershave as he bends close. His hands – long lean fingers, baby-pink nails stroke my cheeks.

It's a happy enough life. Lived under the umbrella of secure jobs and a healthy pension and out of season trips to countries whose names taste like fruit drops on one's tongue.

My illness has no room in such a marriage.

133

∞

A wave of nausea moves through my bones when I think of travelling to Easter Island.

'Have you any idea how long the flight will be?'

Paul listens, pursing his lips and raising his eyebrows.

'We'll travel light, maybe try for an upgrade. And you're looking much better today.'

In bed, he embraces me awkwardly. His shoulders press into my ribcage and I turn away saying I am tired.

'You're always tired.' He turns to his side of bed.

He is blind to my early morning shuffle to the bathroom as I ready myself for another day, slathering my face with foundation and rouge, so that the face smiling back at him looks plump, healthy, and alive. A clown's face.

The cancer started innocently, like a salesman knocking on the wrong door. Suddenly a series of stomach spasms had me bent over in pain.

'It's all this spicy shit you eat,' Paul says, sweeping into the rubbish bin, the sauces and Patak pickles from my Ikea shelves.

At my second visit, the doctor recommends a colonoscopy. I start to nod off when he hands me a plastic jar.

'Some more specimen of my poo? Will it do any good?' I ask.

∞

There are ways of getting better. A world beyond chemo

and drips. I try homeopathy. Little sherbet pills that smell of summer. Every evening I drink a pint of apple cider. One morning I climb three flights of steps to see Mr Zu who holds a first class diploma in acupuncture from Beijing University. I have soft skin that bruises easily, Mr Zu says. His voice has a lisp.

'Your yin and yang forces are not in alignment. Your qi is blocked. Too many knots.'

I tell him there is a constant flutter of wings pressing against my belly button.

He shakes his head and reaches for the little plump tub of Tiger balm on his desk, dips his finger in and rubs his temples gently.

Mr Zu recommends a six-month course of acupuncture to align my spine and kill the tumour

'I accept American Express,' he says. I transfer the money but don't show up. I don't trust his needles.

My next-door neighbour is a healer. I read about her in the local newspaper and decide to pop over. Barbara's skin is pebble smooth. Her plump arms and round hips speak of robust pleasures.

She ushers me into a room where a lone red bulb swings from the ceiling and hands me an A4 laminated sheet with her list of prices. I sit, cross-legged on a batik print beanbag. She clasps my hand in hers and with the other squeezes her left breast. It looks like she's teasing out milk.

'Stop trembling,' she hisses and closes her eyes. A shudder passes through her body. Her shoulders turn rigid and then slacken as though shaking off an unseen weight.

'A constellation of alien cells are attacking each other. Their energy is no good. Your body is like a war zone,' she says. 'You don't have much time.'

'Like Star Wars?' I ask. I feel tired listening to her.

She looks at me but her eyes are hooded and far away.

'Look after the ones you will leave behind,' she says as she shows me to the door.

∞

I make up my mind to get Paul a new wife as the pain continues. I need a substitute. Someone to fill in the blanks and sleep on a bed that still carries the imprint of my absent head. Someone who will laugh at his jokes and remember to buy his favourite whiskey on his birthday.

I think hard before placing the advert. How will I sell my husband? How will I describe the way his blue eyes darken with passion or the mermaid tattoo on his ankle that he hides dutifully behind grey, woollen socks?

'Healthy, scholarly man not yet past his prime, avid voyager seeks an equally healthy, inquisitive female, with a lust for travel and books. Good looks preferred but not essential.' I sign off as James XV.

The advert appears in the newspaper's weekend section of Encounters.

The surgery phones. I have missed two appointments. 'I'm fine. Just fine,' I lie to the receptionist. 'The symptoms have gone.' The truth is I have become addicted to finding my replacement. Every day I trawl the entries on line and in the papers. I play a cat and mouse game with these unknown women. I alone have the power to end their virginal nights. Besides, what is the point of landing in a hospice, the syringes pumping poison into my veins, the pitying look of so-called well-wishers flocking to my bedside?

∞

Not one response pings through the inbox. I tweak Paul's profile adding 'financially comfortable' to his list of virtues.

There is a flood of replies. The world is crowded with healthy, lonely women who love books and are hunting for solvent males. One entry grabs my attention. I get the magnifying glass from Paul's study and hold it close to the photo. Georgie145's cheekbones and the tilt to her eyes could be East European. A Magyar woman from the steppes. Her mouth painted a geisha red is defiant. She wears her lipstick like ammunition. Paul will like that.

She could be Paul's type if he wanted.

Georgie145 writes back saying we should speak over the phone. I aka James XV write back saying I have a bout of laryngitis, and need to rest my throat. It is best to communicate via email.

She has been married before and she loves peacocks, except for their feet. Peacocks have ugly feet, she says, placing five exclamation points after this declaration. I like her humour. It will balance Paul's seriousness. They can fly to Easter Islands together and whilst Paul circles the statues, she can stalk peacocks and clip their toenails.

I arrange to meet Georgie145 in a coffee shop.

'What will you wear? How will I know it's you?' London is swarming with sad and single women. Blink and you will miss them in the gaggle of camera clicking Chinese tourists or rich Arab women dragging their wealth behind them like a poodle.

'I will carry a red pashmina. Will you be in a suit?' She writes back to James XV.

I tell her I will be holding a green golf umbrella.

∞

I do not see Georgie145 immediately. I spot an empty table and sit down, the big green umbrella propped against my shoulder like a drunken parrot.

A hand touches my shoulder. It is Georgie145 wearing her red lipstick.

'You are not Mr James.' She is confused.

'I'll explain everything, but please won't you sit down….'

Georgie145 sits but keeps her coat on.

I place my hand on hers. 'I put the advert for my cousin. He has a wife but she's seriously ill. She won't last long. If you will just win him over. Here, just take a look at his photo.' I fumble in my handbag and bring out an old photo taken on a fishing trip in Mallorca. Paul looks young, earnest and capable.

Her shoulders relax and she edges out of her coat. Georgie145's name is actually Ljubica but she prefers

Georgie. 'It sounds more American,' she says proudly. She is a librarian and the top place on her bucket list is a trip to Easter Island.

She spends the next hour telling me about her childhood in war torn Macedonia.

When I get home, I rush to the bathroom and retch into the bathroom sink. I carefully wipe the blood from the white ceramic.

The bathroom has become a scene of crime. I do not have long.

∞

Georgie145 and I e-mail each other. We meet again. It has been only two weeks, but she says I look changed.

'Is everything okay with you? You don't look well. Is someone taking care of you?'

She will know how to handle Paul's grief when the time comes, hold it carefully like an egg. Nurture it like a mother hen.

I tell her it's just a teeny-weeny flu. I put my hand inside my pocket and fish out a ticket.

'It's for a Tennessee William play, *A Streetcar named Desire*. Her eyes light up. She has already told me she is a fan.

'My cousin will be in the next seat,' I explain.

I lean forward and whisper into her ear what she has to say.

∞

Paul does not want to go to the theatre by himself. I tell him I have migraine and remind him it is his favourite play.

With a cheery goodbye, I nudge him out and curl up in bed, holding the alarm clock in my hand. Soon Paul will slide into his seat and Georgie145 sitting in the next seat will look up and strike up a conversation. He will mumble something about his wife not being able to make it. She will say her friend stood her up. The curtain will go down at interval and they will turn to each other. Georgie145 will say she loves Tennessee Williams.

'Is that so? I researched this play for my PhD dissertation,' Paul will reply, stroking his chin. He will look at her a little more carefully and notice the dimples and the slow burning fire in her deep-set eyes.

'Why don't you tell me a little more about it? You see English is not my first language,' Georgie145 says, lowering her eyes. She will suggest a drink afterwards and Peter will look at his watch.

'Oh... all right then. But just one quick drink, that's all.'

∞

He's back. I check the watch...almost one a.m.

'How was the play?' I ask. Paul has his back to me. 'Not bad,' he says, unbuttoning his shirt. Sliding into bed, he yawns. I move closer, place my hand on his chest. His heart has a quick, frightened beat. Then, out of nowhere he tells me I don't really have to go to Easter Island if I don't feel up to it.

140

'I can find a work colleague to tag along,' he says. His eyes drift away and he stares out the window at the bright lights of a city beckoning.

The Day After

The caterers are gone. The teacups and plates rinsed and put away. Even the red wine spilled on the Turkish rug is blotted dry. The florist places the white lilies on the coffee table, wipes her hands on a tea towel and shuts the kitchen door behind her.

It is the family's turn to leave. The daughter bends down to smooth his wispy flyaway hair. 'You will look after yourself Dad, won't you? Remember to take the warfarin with water,' she says. He sees the lines running down the side of her nose and her thin lips mouthing the instructions. I am the father of an old woman. The thought hits him like a blow. It's the son's turn next. Limp sweaty handshake and a pat, then another, and then another, until he feels his arm being wrenched free from its socket. 'Leave me alone,' he wants to shout, slamming the door on their faces. Instead, he squeezes their hands and says they are not to worry, Mildred, their mum has left his life in tiptop shape.

He stands on the front step, waves them off and goes back in. The house is not his anymore. It is bare-boned and stripped of flesh. It is cold and dark even after he walks through the rooms, switching on the lights, shutting the windows and swivelling the round plastic circle of the thermostat to max. Sitting on the edge of his armchair, he grabs the television remote. The screen jumps to life. It's Mildred's favourite channel. A group of women in bright frocks sit chatting on a sofa. It is all a babbling brook of sound and colour. He puts the radio on. Jeremy Vine is going on about mortgages and PPIs.

The silence is an animal prowling through the rooms.

It is the day after.

Lifting his coat from the hook by the porch, he sets out. The first person he bumps into is Mark, the postman.

'Ah, there you are, Mr. Jones,' Mark says as his hand dives into his bag. He squints at the address before handing him three letters: one from the bank, another from Specsavers and the last, a circular for an Easter egg hunt at the St. John's Unitarian Church.

'I hear she went quickly. No suffering at all,' Mark says as he gives the letters.

'You have a kind face, Mark. The right type of face for a postman,' Mr Jones replies.

Mark nods. He clears his throat. 'Well thank you. Thank you Sir. She was a good lady.'

A slight cough and shuffling of feet and he continues. 'She gave me a lovely bottle last Christmas.'

'Yes, yes... Mildred was daft like that. Say, do you want to pop in and I'll put the kettle on?' Mr Jones asks, moving the letters from one hand to the other. He gives them back to the Mark.

'I'll save these for later. So, what will you have English Breakfast or Darjeeling?'

The postman still has his round to finish. He mumbles something about fresh air and a dog and carries on, Mr

143

Jones's letters back in his bag.

Mr Jones continues walking to the newsagent. He wants a word with Mr Patel about cancelling a subscription. There is no need now for *Knitting and Crochet Made Simple*. Mildred never was a knitter, even though she liked to imagine herself as one. Sitting there by the window, her knitting needles going clackty-clack evening after evening. And what came out at the end- a measly scarf, knit one purl two, the wool already unravelling by the time he'd wrapped it around his neck. The following week she had gone and ruined the scarf in the washing machine. Shouldn't such things be hand washed anyway? But she persisted like a dog with a bone.

He shakes his head. There would be no more knitting no more.

There is Omar the rabbit. He can't remember whether he has fed him before leaving the house. Mildred had the routine written in red felt on the kitchen calendar, ticking off each task with the precision of an engineer. Omar was another one of her impulse purchases. Driving to Morrison's one Tuesday for their weekly shop, she swerved the car sharply to the right towards Ridgeway nursery that along with selling plants also ran OAP coffee mornings and boasted a pet shop on the side.

'Are you trying to kill us? No indicator or horn, just turning like that,' he screamed at her. 'And we don't need any more geraniums, thank you very much.'

'We need a pet not a plant,' she announced grandly, parking the car on a double yellow and marching inside. He

144

had no choice but to follow her.

An hour later, they were pushing their shopping trolley through Morrison's, the rabbit or Omar as she christened him, curled up inside one of the carrier bags. Couldn't she have been more conventional, called him Ollie or Pirate? Pirate would have suited the animal, what with that fuzzy black patch around his left eye.

'Oh, but he is so handsome. Just look at those eyes. They are pure Omar Sharif. He can't be any other name,' Mildred said when he challenged her. Her hands flew up to her cheeks and she squeezed her eyes shut, trying to drag out another name. People milled around them staring as they stood arguing in front of the chilled food cabinet.

'It will have to be Omar,' she said, tucking the rabbit under her arm and striding towards the checkout.

That is how she was. Stubborn like an elephant's leg. It was the same with her illness. He knew she flushed the pills down the loo at night. 'They can't bloody help me, I'm too far gone,' she shouted when he waved the bottle in front of her. No sound of rattling pills. Just silence hitting the plastic. She became so good at giving up on herself.

'Mr Jones. Mr Jones, can I help you?' It is Patel the newsagent, who has come out from behind the till. He stands there stroking his arm like he is some kind of cat.

Mr Jones brushes his hand away. 'I need to cancel the magazine. The knitting magazine for my wife.' His voice comes out, high pitched and shrill. He picks up a packet of jellybeans from the shelf and puts it down again. Spotting the magazine on the second shelf, he rummages around in his pocket for his wallet. He has left it at home. He blames Mildred. Always nosing around his stuff, turning his trousers inside out, fishing out the loose coins and unfolding his twenty-pound bills. She would lay them flat on the table and count them out slowly. 'That's two twenties, dear. Mind you don't blow them on some floozy.' There would be a chuckle and a wink.

Mr Jones shakes his head.

'I've come for the magazine but I've left my wallet at home.'

'Don't worry about it, Mr Jones,' Patel says. 'You can pay next time.' He presses the *Knitting and Crochet Made Simple* into his hand.

Patel has kind eyes too. The world is full of kind eyed men going about their business with a smile.

'You are a gentleman Patel. Won't you come home and have some tea?' Mr Jones hears himself say. That is a first. Inviting a stranger into his home. What would Mildred say?

Patel's mouth opens round like a circle and then folds back into a u-shaped smile. He has strong healthy teeth. 'Thank you, Mr Jones. Thank you. Maybe another time.' Eyelids lowered, he tilts his chin towards the cash register.

Mr Jones is already shuffling towards the door, the magazine safely tucked under his armpit. He stops outside the shop and steadies himself on the front step, holding the railing. His shoelaces are undone, but he can't be bothered to bend down and tie them.

'Mr Jones. Wait!'

Somebody is running after him. It is the little man Patel again, wringing his hands, eyes cloudy and shiny with tears.

'Is it about Mildred?' Mr Jones asks.

'I heard the news. So sorry for your loss. She was a true lady.' Mr Patel bows his head.

'It is what it is, young man. With those kind eyes you can conquer the world.' Mr Jones comforts Patel, jabbing him on the shoulder with his index finger.

Out on the street he looks at the sky. It is turning out to be a fine day. He decides to go to a park and eat his sandwich. Mildred will go mad, but he does not give a damn. The sun is out and he refuses to spend the afternoon hunched over the kitchen table, spooning her defrosted potato leek soup into his mouth, the Archers blaring from the radio. The soup will be too watery and salty. God, she was a lousy cook. She had confessed as much on their wedding day.

'I promise to boil you an egg, every day of my life.' That was her wedding day promise. Her minty breath fanning his cheek as they stood hand in hand at the Bayswater Registry. And the Registrar, Smith or was it Anderson... he can't place the name, pale fellow with a big double chin had beamed while he grinned from ear to ear, weak with laughter and love.

'A boiled egg!' Mr Jones snorts at the memory. He remembers it all. The early days. They had gone to

Blackpool for their honeymoon. She wanted Verona. 'To walk in the footsteps of Romeo and Juliet and eat gelato,' she had whispered with dreamy eyes. 'We'll go one day when there's money,' he promised her, his voice gruff with disappointment. They spent the week huddled in love inside the bedsit. Sneaking out in the evening, avoiding the landlady's watchful eye, he smuggled in a portion of fish and chips. They ate in bed, licking the salty grease off each other's fingers. Mildred's long dark hair speckled with golden breadcrumbs the next morning. Afterwards she had pouted and said, 'You never even showed me the Pier.'

Mr Jones smiles at the memory.

'Oy, get a move on. You can't just stand in the middle of the road.' A bell rings and a cyclist glowers at him from beneath his helmet, his yellow Lycra body quivering in rage.

The park is lovely this time of day, Mr Jones observes crossing into the park. He feels the tremor of spring in the trees. The tremble of branches breaking into bud. Nodding approval at the flowerbeds packed tight with chrysanthemum, he walks to a bench near the pond. It is occupied, but he does not mind. The girls sitting there shift closer to give him room. They are taking photos of each other on their mobiles, pouting lips, tongues sticking out, but all he sees are their round cheeks flushed pink in the cold air and the healthy shine of their hair that spills like a waterfall on their maroon school blazers.

'You have beautiful faces,' Mr Jones tells them. 'My daughter was like you.' He sighs and stares at the pond before continuing. 'Look at her now. Full of worry. Can't remember the last time she laughed.' He turns to the girl sitting nearest to him and tweaks her cheek. 'Don't ever lose the bloom.'

They get up and walk away. Except for one. The prettiest one. She stands over him, hands on her hip and spits out gum at his shoes. 'Sick old perv. Go die,' she hisses and snatches his magazine, rolls it into a tube and flings it into the pond.

He watches it fly through the air, hears the soft plop as it hits the water. Instead of yelling at them, he shakes his head. He will just have to buy Mildred another.

'Don't ever lose the bloom,' he murmurs again, watching the girl as she runs off to join her friends.

Mildred was never the mothering kind. Anna and James grew by themselves. Like trees in a forest. Took themselves off to school and then university. It was her constitution. Always feeble. She caught a cold just putting the wheelie bins out on a Tuesday. She blamed her Irish childhood.

'Mam only fed us potatoes and soup,' she used to say when they began courting. 'My insides just curled up and died. I am no good for the daily grind.'

He was not upset. He wanted her just the way she was. The day he first saw her, standing at the traffic lights in her green paisley skirt, hesitating to cross the road. He ran up to her, unfurling his umbrella to cover her.

'Miss, Miss,' he'd called out. 'You don't want to spoil that lovely hair in the rain.'

She had thrown him her special look, blue eyes sparkling behind the dark fringe of her lashes. He made up his mind. She was the one.

His stomach rumbles. He has forgotten to buy a sandwich. He looks around him. The park is empty and the lights have come on. He cannot see the schoolgirls. He wants to have a word with them about their manners but they are nowhere. A breeze sets up and he starts to shiver.

It is time to go home.

Nearing his house, Mr Jones spots the schoolgirl standing alone at the bus stop. He recognises her. She's the one who threw away Mildred's magazine. He walks up to her. Her head is bent over the blue screen of her mobile, her fingers busy stabbing into it. Swiftly, before she's even realised it, he grabs the mobile from her hand and throws it as far as he can.

'What the hell!' The girl lets out a wail and scampers after it, running across the road.

'There, that'll teach you to mess with my Mildred's things,' he says, walking away, rubbing his hands together in satisfaction.

His house is all lit up like the Blackpool illuminations. The front door wide open. A huddle of people stand in the porch. He sees the rabbit scurrying down the driveway.

'Omar, Omar come back.' He whistles but it disappears under the garden hedge before he can catch it.

'Dad! Dad, where have you been?' His daughter runs towards him. The postman and Mr Patel, the newsagent are right behind her, shaking their heads. 'We were so worried about you,' they say, taking hold of his elbow and guiding him into the house.

He stares at them. 'Have you dropped in for tea?'

'You need to sit down. Take it easy,' his daughter says, seating him at the kitchen table and pushing a bowl of defrosted leek soup towards him.

'It's been a long day,' Mr Jones says. He takes off his jacket. Outside, through the open window, he spots a scatter of stars in the sky. One spirals out of control, blinking brighter than the rest.

He gets up to take a closer look, craning his head out the window to have a better view. There she is. His Mildred. Sparkling like a diamond.

'I'll be alright, my love,' he shouts.

Cookery Lessons in Suburbia

The first time I meet Mrs Kim is at the school bus stop. I smile and extend my hand. 'Hello, I'm Mrs Murthy and this is my granddaughter Maya. I come over every year from India to help my daughter with child care.'

'I am Mrs Kim and this is Christina. She is also my granddaughter,' she says in return.

Mrs Kim is small, probably in her sixties. She's dressed smartly in a tweed skirt as though she is going to an office. There are blue shadows under her eyes, like puddles of still water.

'Is Christina your friend?' I ask my granddaughter when she's back from school. She screws up her nose, her mouth busy chewing gum, her eyes lost in the shiny television screen.

'She's not my friend. She's not cool. Adam Cohen is not inviting her to his Bar Mitzvah.'

'Her grandmother told me she's a Grade 6 in piano,' I say in Christina's defence.

Maya's little shoulders lift, dismissing this achievement.

Every morning I check the calendar, cross off the days until I can fly back to my old life in India, to my sleepy town by the sea where the biggest excitement is the arrival of the Moscow State circus every winter. I miss my town Thirupuram or TP as my granddaughter calls it. I tell her to practice saying the name, but she simply shakes her head

152

and says it sounds weird like some disease.

'Your mother was born in TP. She will tell you about the house with its courtyard and the peepal tree in the middle.' Maya is not interested in my stories or my food. She prefers chicken drumsticks and pizzas and she turns up her nose when I prepare rice appam for dinner. I use fresh curry leaves, grated coconut chutney and slivers of green and red chillies that I decorate on the side in the shape of a flower. At least my daughter's face lights up when she sees her childhood favourites.

'Home made yoghurt too,' she squeals in delight, slumping into her chair, rubbing the bridge of her nose where her glasses have left red bruise marks like insect bites.

'You work too hard,' I tell her, ladling some more sambar into her bowl.

'This is America, Ma. Everyone works hard. It's not your sweet Thirupuram where dad can come home for idli dosa and enjoy a two hour siesta and then have his Brooke Bond tea and read the papers.'

I change the topic. 'I met a Chinese lady today at the school bus stop,' I tell her. I want her to know I've made a friend.

'That must be Mrs Kim? She's Korean, Ma. She moved here from Texas a couple of weeks back.' My daughter is on the neighbourhood watch scheme and knows about such things.

'Do you know her children? I saw her with a little girl, her granddaughter, Christina.'

My daughter sighs and starts fiddling with her hair, curling one loose strand around her index finger. It melts my heart seeing her like this.

'Mrs Kim's a sad case, Ma. She lost her daughter in a car crash and now looks after little Christina. She has a son too. He's in his twenties, but more like a little boy.'

'What's wrong with him? Is he spastic?' I ask.

'You can't use that word these days.' My daughter scowls, giving me an impatient look. She taps the side of her head with her right index finger.

'He's on the Autistic spectrum, Ma. He can be a bit funny at times,' she says. 'Mrs Kim tends to keep to herself. I'm surprised she came up to you and said hello.'

∞

I dream of Mrs Kim that night. She floats in the air, her arms thrashing as she swims after her daughter and her son who remain always out of reach. The next morning my pillow is soaked with tears.

I want to invite Mrs Kim home for tea. Mostly out of the goodness of my heart, but I also want to find out a little more about her son's Spectrum business. My husband is a homeopath and I carry with me a little black box full of his specialist pills. Maybe they can help his condition.

The following week, seeing Mrs Kim at the bus stop, I extend my invitation. She looks puzzled. She rolls up her cardigan sleeve and looks at her watch and then at me. 'Tea? With you? Why?' Her voice is doubtful.

'Because we are friends.' I smile.

'I don't know you, but I will come. Where do you live?' Mrs Kim asks in her straightforward manner.

I point to my daughter's red roofed house at the end of the street.

'It's the biggest house on the street. You can't miss it.' My chest puffs out in pride.

She bows and says thank you.

'Please bring your son too,' I call after her, but she is walking away and doesn't hear me.

I prepare north Indian snacks for tea. They will suit Mrs Kim's Chinese palette. First, the samosas-I unfurl the short crust pastry on the kitchen counter, dusting it with flour and cutting it into triangles. I sauté onions, ginger and freshly shelled peas in the pan along with boiled potatoes which I slide into the little triangles folds. Next, come the chicken cutlets. I fry them in batches, making sure to keep at least a dozen aside for Maya. I'm just finishing the banana fritters, adding the last of cardamom to the mix when the doorbell rings.

There she stands, resplendent in a blue tweed jacket and smart patent leather shoes with heels, a bunch of roses in her hand, a string of pearls around her neck.

'You look so smart Mrs Kim, like an airhostess,' I say, smoothing the pleats of my Kanjeevaram silk sari. I've also made an effort to dress elegantly for our meeting. I usher her in, and watch with pride as her eyes take in the imported Italian cream leather sofa and the 20-inch television hanging above the mantelpiece.

'My son-in-law is a doctor and my daughter is in IT. They have important jobs,' I inform Mrs Kim. It is better to share this basic information right away. One is then ready to talk of deeper things. Like finding a cure for her son's illness for example. Mrs Kim nods, but she offers no family details of her own. She's still holding the roses. I take them and put them in a crystal vase on the dining table. 'I'll add the water afterwards,' I say, nudging her towards the kitchen.

The granite counters in the kitchen have been polished twice and the stainless steel sink gleams like a mirror. The kitchen is the soul of the house and I want to make sure everything is first-class. I have even lit an apple scented Yankee candle to get rid of the curry fragrance.

Mrs Kim sniffs slightly as though trying to detect a bad smell. I point her towards the kitchen table, which I've covered with an embroidered white table cloth.

'Please take a seat.'

'First time I am eating your kind of food,' she says sliding into her chair.

'You're in for a treat,' I assure her.

I put four samosas on my daughter's best rose patterned plate and place it in front of Mrs Kim like an offering. She dabs her mouth with the edge of her napkin, shuts her eyes and mutters a prayer in her mother tongue. 'Just a little thank you to God,' she explains and begins cutting the samosas into little bite sized pieces with her knife, her forehead pink with concentration. There is silence as we eat together. Not the bone-heavy stillness that greets me when I come back to an empty home after dropping Maya to the bus stop. This silence is warm and cosy like between friends.

'So what do you think?' I ask her after she's finished the samosa. 'Do you like my food? My husband says there is magic in my fingers.' I stop myself. It's rude to boast in front of guests.

She hesitates. 'Very nice, but too spicy. The puff pastry is too thick also,' she says.

'That's why I give you the yoghurt.' I point to the small terracotta bowl near her plate. 'This will cool your tongue.' I ignore her comment about the puff pastry.

'I like banana fritters the best,' Mrs Kim announces, pushing her empty plate towards me for seconds. The gold yellow crumbs glisten on her small rosebud of a mouth.

She looks around the kitchen. Her eyes rest on the wall with the family photos. I point to the one where my daughter is posing on the Great Wall of China, squinting at the camera, dressed like an athlete in a tracksuit and trainers.

'See, that is my daughter. She's in China. She travels a lot for work. That is why I am here, to help with Maya when she is away. A free maid!' I laugh to make it sound jokey. I don't want Mrs Kim to think I'm complaining.

'I'm from Korea, not China,' she says and frowns. I rush in to smooth matters. 'Yes, of course. Different country. But you like Chinese food, no?' I'm embarrassed.

'Have you eaten Bulgogi and kimchi?' She asks. Her face is expectant.

I shake my head. 'I eat chop suey and sweet and sour chicken. On Sundays, my daughter likes to order a takeout from Peking Palace.'

'Oh, eating restaurant food. Is no good.' Her mouth curls in disdain. 'Maybe I'll call you home one day to try my food.' A shadow passes over Mrs Kim's face when she says this.

I want specifics. A date and a time. One day is not good enough. It sounds open-ended and meaningless, like the 'have a great day,' shouted by the saleswomen in shopping malls.

'Let me show you how I make chutney, so you can make it at home.' I get up and take out the coconut from the fridge. I show her the special serrated knife I have brought from Thirupuram. 'Sharp as a scorpion's sting,' I say, running my finger over the blade. 'It's our family knife. My mother gave it to me. I will leave it behind for my daughter.' The thought makes me sad, because I know she will have no time to grind ginger, grate coconut, or slice through the soft belly of a gourd. My daughter will spend her life sitting behind a desk staring at a computer screen and ordering take away pizzas. The knife will stay untouched in the kitchen drawer.

'American knives no good. Too soft,' Mrs Kim agrees. It turns out she has a special Korean knife too. 'For slicing beef. It cuts it thin like flower petals. Korean food is like making art. I will cook you some beef.'

I'm about to tell her I don't eat beef when her cell phone flashes. She says something in Korean and starts collecting her jacket and her keys.

'I must go now.' She almost jogs towards the door. I remember her son.

'Take some food for your son,' I say, spooning the fritters into the plastic disposable container my daughter bulk buys from Costco every month. I press it into her hands.

Mrs Kim's shoulders stiffen. Her upper lip is beaded with sweat. 'Who tell you about my son?' she asks. The blue shadows under her eyes seem to throb and bleed onto her cheeks.

'Everyone knows you have a son,' I say, making light of it. 'A lovely boy,' I add. I've never seen him but isn't this what all mothers like to hear.

She hands me back the Tupperware. 'My son only likes my cooking.'

'No, please take it.' My voice is firm.

In her haste to leave, Mrs Kim leaves her handbag behind. I notice it as I am clearing the table. Resisting the urge to unzip it and look inside, I swing it over my arm and go out to find her. Mrs Kim's house is the last one in the cul de sac. It's a modest house with yellow lace curtains in the window. A wind chime sways from the magnolia tree near the front door and rows of cheerful blue gnomes stand on each red brick step. I ring the doorbell and when no one answers, I peep in through the window. There she sits, Mrs Kim on a battered brown sofa, her smart jacket still on. Next to her is a young man, round shouldered and unshaven. He wears a white vest that seems spattered with food stains. His blue pyjamas bottoms have a teddy bear print. She pats his cheek and bending down picks up my Tupperware, opens the lid, lifts the orange gooey fritter and tenderly as one would feed a baby, brings it to the man's mouth. He claps his hands. Mrs Kim's face softens, the harsh plane of her cheeks seem to melt away and her eyes turn all dreamy. She shifts closer to him, her arm encircling his shoulders and wipes his mouth with a lacy handkerchief. I leave the handbag on the front step and quickly walk away. That night I tell my daughter that Mrs Kim loved my food.

∞

Weeks pass but there is no return invitation from Mrs Kim. Soon it will be time for me to fly back home. Mrs Kim is now always late for the school bus. She breaks into a run when she sees the yellow bus nosing its way down the street. Waving frantically, she pushes her granddaughter up the steps and mops her forehead. The blue shadows under her eyes seem to get deeper and deeper. It is clear she has no time for my friendship. Then one evening, my daughter has news for me. Mrs Kim's son has run away and the police can't find him anywhere. I decide to visit Mrs Kim. She will need a friend in this time of sorrow.

Mrs Kim answers the doorbell. Her blouse is wrinkled. A stained and dirty gingham apron encircles her boyish gaunt hips and her neat bob is bunched into an untidy ponytail. She blinks rapidly and shields her eyes from the sun.

'Oh, it's only you.' Her smile fades as she lets me in.

The house reeks with a pungent smell.

'Are you cooking?' I put on my brightest voice. Maybe her son's disappearance is a rumour and he's safely back home.

'Yes, yes, come in...' Her voice is distracted. She is breathing hard. The living room is small and shabby. I notice the wheelchair and the plastic bowls filled with food that sit on the coffee table. A large bib with 'Ji Ho' embroidered in swirly letters lies on the sofa armrest.

'Our granddaughters are friends,' I remind her. This is a lie. Maya refuses to talk to Christina, despite my repeated attempts to tell her that all immigrants must stick together.

'I'm making kimchi,' Mrs Kim says. 'Follow me. I show you.'

'That's wonderful. I'll teach you how to make mango pickle in exchange,' I say. I'm all for quid pro quo.

'Not needed,' she says rudely. 'No one like mango in this house.'

The kitchen is old fashioned with peeling paint on the walls and Formica cabinets that have chipped corners. A large framed poster of a smiling bald man in a black jacket, holding a bible in his hand dominates one wall. I imagine him to be Mrs Kim's late husband. The shredded cabbage with the garlic is already in the plastic mixing bowl. She lifts her Korean knife and starts slicing the scallions and the ginger. Her fingers move nimbly like mice scampering after cheese.

'I heard about your son. I'm sorry,' I tell her.

Mrs Kim's mouth remains set and her hands slicing the ginger halt for an instant before resuming the cutting.

'Ji Ho wants to see the world. Always. He cries that I keep him indoors like a prisoner.' She shakes her head and blinks furiously, glancing at me before continuing.

'Tell me what's there to see in this America? He will go to McDonalds. He will eat some tasteless round meat inside some old white bread buns, go to the shopping mall and people will point. They will giggle. All bullshit.' The words rush out of her mouth like a waterfall. 'Ji Ho will be back. You will see. He needs his mother. He needs my food.' Her mouth twists into an ugly grimace when she says this.

I reach out and touch her shoulder but she flicks away my hand and goes back to stirring the kimchi, drizzling brown sugar into what looks like a dark, coagulating mess.

'This is special,' Mrs Kim says. 'It's fermented for nearly six months. Makes it more.' She pauses and pulls at her ponytail, as though to tease out the right word and giving up reaches for the English Korean dictionary on the windowsill.

'Makes it TART,' she says, her index finger resting on the open page. 'My son prefers it like this.'

'You must love your son, Ji Ho.' I am ashamed as soon as I say it. 'My husband is a homeopath doctor. He can cure everything.' I continue.

'That is more bullshit. Nothing wrong with my son,' she snorts and starts spooning the mixture into a delicate porcelain bowl. Next to it, she puts little diamond-shaped mounds of boiled rice topped with a lacy green of scallion shoots.

Head lowered and muttering a little prayer, she places the food on a lacquer tray but her hands aren't steady and the bowls seem to slide this way and that. I rush forward and grab the tray. She tells me to follow her into the living room and put the tray on the table next to the wheelchair where it joins other bowls of similar looking food.

I look at the bowls properly this time. There is fruit – crescent cut oranges and little wheels of kiwi looking dull and shrivelled. A sheen of brown covers everything. Little Verdi-Gris mould springs out of the congealed rice and the aroma that I had mistaken for soya sauce is the stench of decaying fish heads that nestle among the rice. Their dead eyes, the colour of sea washed stone, stare back at me.

Mrs Kim stands near me, wiping her hands on her apron, her eyes bright with satisfaction as she checks the fruits of her labour. Her eyes dart from one bowl to another. She nods as though ticking off items on an inventory. 'All Ji Ho's favourite foods. I cook fresh every day, so he can enjoy them when he comes home.' She bows and sweeps her arm wide and begins swaying on the balls of her feet. 'It's all here,' she repeats, in a high-pitched voice. 'All my little boy's favourites – Hoeddeok, Bulgogi, Samgyeopsal, Japchae.' She recites the dishes, looking straight through me, straight into her past where she sits with her son in the kitchen feeding him her food.

Shutting her front door softly behind me, I run back to

my daughter's house as fast as my ageing legs will carry me. I spend the day cleaning the fridge, emptying it of old food and take a cab to the farmer's market where everything costs double that of Walmart. I fill my bag to the brim with vine-ripened tomatoes, plump aubergines and fish whose gills palpitate with life. That night I prepare a feast for my daughter who will be returning home tired and grumpy.

When Maya comes to my room to wish me good night, I throw my arms around her and start weeping, my head pressed against the little puzzled tripping of her heart. She smooths my hair, pats my head, and says in a grown-up type of voice.

'You are missing grandpa, I know. I think it's time you went back to India.'

∞

I return to America the following year. Everything is as it was before except that Mrs Kim or Christina are no longer at the bus stop. I walk past their house but the wind chimes and the gnomes have disappeared and a large blue trampoline sits in the front yard.

'Where is Mrs Kim? Did her son come back?' I ask my daughter.

She knits her brow and screws up her face as though remembering something unpleasant.

'Oh, it's all very sad. Mrs Kim doesn't live here anymore. A young family bought her house and social services have placed Christina with a foster family. She goes to a different school, other side of town. Poor little girl.'

I feel my mouth go dry.

'What did Mrs Kim do? Where is she?'

'It all started when Christina told her teacher about her granny. How she stayed up all night cooking and god knows what for her uncle. Everyone knew he was missing, so the teacher naturally alerted the police who went round. They found Mrs Kim stark naked in the kitchen, stirring a pot of octopus or some other disgusting thing. The house was stinking. I mean it was a health hazard.' She curls up her nose. 'All for a dead man.'

'Dead?' I raise my voice to stop her continuing. 'Did you say Ji Ho has died?'

She looks at me suspiciously. 'You know his name…? Yes, Ji Ho was electrocuted on the railway tracks. Apparently, Mrs Kim used to lock him indoors and beat him if he disobeyed her. One day, he stole her key and wandered out.'

I keep my voice steady and ask her for more details.

'You're getting nosy in your old age, Ma,' my daughter says in an affectionate voice before continuing.

'They found him finally. It was a few months after you had gone back to India. Some people spotted him near the railway station. He was like a tramp, with tattered clothes and a long beard. They asked him where he lived, but he didn't have a clue. I think he was trying to come back home. His ankle became trapped in the railway tracks as he was crossing. The train could not stop in time. They identified him because of the little identity chain around his neck. It had his name.'

'And Mrs Kim?' I can barely speak. I place my right hand on top of my left to stop it shaking.

'She went back to Korea, Ma. She kicked up a big fuss about the son, though. I remember that, she wanted to take his body back draped in the Korean flag. It was all highly stressful. It even made the evening news. Anyway, enough of poor Mrs Kim.'

She bends towards me and kisses my cheek. I smell the lemon-yellow shampoo scent of her hair.

'We're so happy you're back, Ma. Will you make some rice appam for me tonight? Please?'

Springtime in Japan

Sitting on the edge of his hotel bed, shoulders hunched forward, the Samsung Galaxy pressed against his ear, Dr Basu waits for his wife's voice.

'What took you so long, Asha?' He asked.

'I was outside, pruning the roses,' she replies.

'How do the roses look?'

She laughs. 'You're being silly Dr Basu. You remember them perfectly well. You've only been gone a few days you know.'

Married for thirty-five years but she still refuses to call him by his first name Kallol. Maybe it was to do with his academic post, a history professor of Egyptology at the university.

Dr Basu remembers his garden. On summer evenings, he liked to sit on the patio, the sun washing his face while he sipped his Yorkshire tea and read *The English Historical Review*. Two crescent shaped rose beds took pride of place. They chose the roses together, his wife and him, pouring over the Peter Beales Rose Catalogue. The roses were there to commemorate their silver wedding anniversary and Asha fussed over them, as she would've over a child if they'd ever had one.

'Have you heard about this new virus from China?' Dr Basu asks his wife over the phone.

Asha laughs. 'Oh that! People overreact. It is just a flu as far as I'm concerned. It can't be worse than malaria.'

Dr Basu smiles. He liked his wife's spirit. The way she had plucked herself from a city like Calcutta and replanted her roots in Woodford -a quiet English town where the grey rain drip dripped like laundry drying on a clothesline.

'Be careful, Asha,' he repeats. He had sensed a change at the Ancient Egyptian Materials and Treasures International Conference in Shenzuban. The BBC World Service reported of an Epidemic. It was all very worrying Dr Basu thinks sitting on the hotel bed in his striped navy blue pyjamas talking to his wife in England whilst the sky outside his window goes indigo black. He can't spot a single star.

Dr Merton, his colleague from the university who had accompanied him to Japan for the conference, is worried too. He glances over his shoulder, before lowering his voice. 'We're not far from the epicentre you know.'

'I hope the conference is not cut short,' Dr Basu replies. He was presenting a paper on *Temples, Ritual, and Mourning Symbolism in the Ancient World* and was speaking on the last day.

'I've still not seen much of the city,' he continues. Dr Basu had hoped for Tokyo, instead the organisers had moved the conference to Shenzuban where the local attractions included a Micky Mouse shaped ice skating rink and an eighteenth century Shinto shrine dedicated to the sun goddess Amaterasu.

They stand side by side in the conference cafeteria, holding out their black lacquer trays like schoolboys. The conference is a triumph for Dr Basu. He was nearing retirement and to be invited to present a keynote paper to academic colleagues was an honour he couldn't have refused. He wanted Asha to accompany him. Several of the delegates had brought their spouses and a separate cultural programme was drawn up for them - trips to the Shinto temple, a tea drinking ceremony and a kimono tying class. But Asha was not interested. 'I'm happy here with my roses, besides I can't let the Parish down,' she said, her brown eyes calm and steady behind her round glasses. She patted his cheek lightly,

'You go Dr Basu. You've been working on that research paper for years and you've never been to Japan.'

Once a week Asha Basu drove to Woodford St. George's Parish Church where she chatted with a group of Somali women, mostly asylum seekers, helping them with their English. Dr Basu marvelled at this interconnectedness of the world. Here was his wife teaching Wordsworth to Somali women in a draughty parish room with posters of Jesus feeding lambs.

'My wife is teaching English to some Somali women, that's why she couldn't come here,' Dr Basu confides to Dr Merton in the lunch queue.

'Isn't that just splendid,' Dr Merton says. 'I wish Sue did something useful like that but our grandchildren keep her occupied.' He sighs, but it is a happy kind of sigh, Dr Basu

169

thinks. It says look at me, my Family Tree will continue to flourish long after you and your childless wife are a fistful of ash on some funeral pyre.

'Well, it's pork ramen again,' Dr Basu changes the topic. He whispers this because he didn't want to offend the serving ladies who stand behind the glass topped counter, smartly dressed in their black skirts and white aprons. Their patent shoes shine like mirrors.

'Are you going to stick to your bread rolls and butter?' Dr Merton raises an amused eyebrow.

Dr Basu nods. 'As a vegetarian I don't really have much choice do I?' He feels a pang for his wife's cauliflower curry with its tease of cumin, ginger and chillies winking like red rubies among the white florets.

Dr Basu rings his wife to tell her he had dreamt of her cauliflower dish.

'That's the first thing I'll cook for you when you come home,' she promises.

'I'll just have to adjust to this diet. Not long to go before I'm back.' Dr Basu looked at his Seiko watch. A few more days of eating bread rolls and drinking green tea. 'Why can't they make normal tea with teabags and milk? And no Mcvities biscuits either.'

His wife chuckled. 'I should have packed you some teabags and your favourite chocolate digestives. I was sure you would find them in Japan'

This was not modern Japan, Dr Basu explained again to his wife. This was Shenzuban, a small town with a

170

population of four thousand.

∞

On the sixth day of the conference, the mood became
sombre. The local staff tiptoe between the different meeting
rooms, their heads bowed and arms folded behind their
backs. A leaflet appears, perched on top of Dr. Basu's hotel
pillow like a bird. It states he must wear a mask inside the
conference hall. A conspiratorial murmur passes through
the delegates like the susurration of the wind among the
trees. Two Italian tourists in Tokyo had fallen ill with the
virus. The head of the history department at Shenzuban
University holds an emergency meeting, 'Esteemed
colleagues,' he says, his Adam's apple moving with emotion.

'We must be vigilant. Please hold on to your health and
sanity.'

Dr Merton and Dr Basu sitting side by side in the last
row giggle and nudge each other. 'Sanity! Something's lost
in translation, surely.'

Two young girls wearing white gloves hand out
disposable masks from a silver platter. 'The spouse
programme has been scrapped,' Dr Merton murmurs on the
way to the cafeteria. 'Good job our Sue and Asha did not
bother coming.'

In the dining hall, they find prepacked disposable bento
boxes with cellophane wrapped sandwiches, an apple and a
carton of green tea.

'The situation is changing quickly,' Dr Basu phones his

wife and explains. Was England the same?' he asked.

'Nothing to worry here,' Asha replies. The parish were taking the Somali ladies to Blackpool and she would be accompanying them. 'Isn't it amazing Dr Basu,' she said, 'These poor women crossed the sea in rubber dinghies afraid for their life and now they'll be picnicking on the beach. Imagine their delight.'

Dr Basu missed her. It was an ache that travelled from his toes, to his knees, past his thighs, groin and belly button before settling inside his ribcage where it swelled like a balloon.

'I wish I could come back soon. The food here is most unsatisfactory,' he complains.

'There must be some Indian restaurant in town. Some enterprising fellow from Gujrat would have set up shop. Stop sulking Dr Basu. Go outside, investigate,' his wife suggests.

Dr Basu considers this. He's tired of watching Japanese dubbed reruns of Perry Mason on TV. Asha was right. It was time to take in the flavour of the town.

The following day he requests a map from the reception and goes out. He begins with the Shinto shrine. A pair of jade green statues of foxes guard the entrance. Walking under the orange arched torii, he feels a sense of calm. Two old women stand with bowed heads and folded hands in front of an elaborate stone trough filled with white lotus blooms and long incense sticks. The incense smoke makes Dr Basu's eyes itch. He sits down on a bench. A bald headed monk in red robes approaches him and pulls out a few folded paper slips from deep within the pleats of his robe. 'Please choose and read.' He holds them out.

'Sorry, I don't read Japanese.' Dr Basu picks one and glances at the paper. He is about to hand it back when he notices that the writing is in English as well. *Daikyo or Great Bad Luck Will Soon Greet You*, he reads it out loudly and slowly.

'I don't like this message. Can I pick another?' He gives back the slip to the monk who shakes his head, refusing to take it. He tells Dr Basu to follow him to the pine tree near the archway.

Pink and cream paper slips similar to the one he is holding dangle from the branches, swaying on strings in the afternoon haze. They remind Dr Basu of the butterflies that flutter over his roses back home in Woodford.

'You tie your *omikuji* here. You leave your bad fortune behind.' The monk smiles and extends his right palm. 'That will be fifty American dollars to get rid of your bad luck.'

'Fifty dollars. How gullible can you be, Dr Basu,' Asha says when he tells her about his trip to the temple.

'Consider it charity. Besides I didn't want to bring that bad luck with me,' Dr Basu pacifies her.

'I've found you your Indian restaurant,' Dr Merton tells him a few days into the conference. 'The Trip Advisor gave it two stars.'

Dr Basu nods. 'I'll go there tonight.'

A fine drizzle had set in and the streets were mostly quiet

when he steps out. Brightly lit public buses drove quietly carrying their cargo of bent figures, faces muffled beneath masks and scarves. Neon lit signs on top of concrete buildings advertised Sapporo beer and Shiroi Koibito Biscuits. Dr Basu stopped a cyclist idling near a drinks kiosk and asked directions to Jaipur Palace.

He finds the restaurant after three false turns. The décor reminds Dr Basu of the Bangladeshi restaurants in Woodford. There was the same wooden beaded curtain hiding the kitchen and black and white prints of Taj Mahal. A blue and red tapestry embroidered with an image of Mt. Fuji hung above the Formica counter where three bottles of Suntory Whisky stood proudly along with bowls of Polo mints and scented fennel seeds.

Biku Patel, the café owner greeted him like a long lost relative. The restaurant was empty so he has plenty of time to chat. How long was Dr Basu there for and why hadn't he brought his Mrs? Did his university job pay well? The barrage of questions accompanies Dr Basu as he ate his food - two bowls of black dal, cauliflower curry and one garlic naan.

'The food is good,' he tells Patel, as he waits for him to tot up the bill. Biku Patel bows, pressing his hand on his heart. 'This is on the house, Sir.' He slides two samosas in a brown paper bag. 'For a fellow countryman.'

'Thank you.' Dr Bose notes the restaurant's name and address in the little maroon leather notebook he carries in the top pocket of his jacket.

On the way back to the hotel, he takes a wrong turn and finds himself in an alley crowded with boarded up shops and graffiti on the walls. Trashcans spilled over with fish bones and rotting vegetables. Lying in the shadow of a doorway is a dog with soft brown fur the colour of his lounge carpet. Dr Basu rummages in his pocket and pulls out the paper bag with the samosas. 'Here doggy, here.' He throws one samosa towards the dog like a ball. The dog gets up slowly and limps towards the samosa. Dr Basu sees that his right hind leg is twisted and a patch of dried blood sticks to his fur.

'Poor little thing, are you as lost as me?' He crouches down and strokes the dog's head. The dog winces, bares his fangs and steps back before wagging his tail softly and following him as he makes his way back to the hotel.

Dr Basu tells his wife about the restaurant and the dog when he is back in the hotel room.

'Since when have you liked dogs? Maybe we can get a pet when you get back,' she suggests.

'We're too old for all the fuss and caring it would require. Anyway how was your trip to Blackpool?' he asks.

It was a cold, blustery day in Blackpool, his wife told him. They had queued for fish and chips and some women had wanted to go on the Big Dipper.

'Like a fool I left my coat at home,' Mrs Basu says. 'I was shivering the whole day.'

Dr Basu wakes up to another newsletter slipped under his door. The first case of the infection has reached the city. A sales representative was taken ill on the night bus from Tokyo and was now isolated in the hospital. The warning is in capital letters. 'MASKS COMPULSORY. NO SHAKING HANDS.'

'They're overreacting surely,' Dr Basu wants reassurance but Merton frowns and says he'd phoned home and advised his wife to stock up on toilet rolls and Heinz chicken soup.

'How was the curry house anyway?' He asks.

'It was okay but the owner was far too talkative. Kept asking all these intrusive questions.' Dr Basu remembers the dog. 'Actually I made a new friend.'

'Don't tell me you found yourself a geisha! What's her name? Suzie Wong?' Merton taps the side of his nose. 'You're a dark horse, you are.'

'It's a dog,' Basu answers stiffly. 'It followed me back to the hotel. I think he likes me.'

They are summoned to the conference hall. The chairman enquires if they've seen the news. Heads nod. Measures were being taken, the cleaning rota was increased and ...on and on does his voice drone. Dr Basu's neck and eyelids feel heavy. He glances outside the window. The maple and beech trees stand forlorn and naked. A weak yellow sun hangs like a solitary light bulb in the sky. Dr Basu imagines the greyness of the day swallowing him whole. He needs fresh air.

Outside, the sharp March wind stings him. He pushed his hands deep inside his tweed jacket. A flash of brown near the lamppost catches his eye. 'Hello dog,' he calls out. The dog comes to him, whimpers and licks his outstretched hand. He is dragging his leg. The blotch of red that Dr Basu had noticed earlier has expanded, covering most of its haunch.

Dr Basu remembers the bread rolls in his room. He can't bear to eat them or throw them away. He goes up to his room and is soon outside again, feeding the dog. A few passers-by shake their head and frown seeing him do this. The hotel receptionist comes out and informs him that it was against Japanese policy to feed stray dogs. 'They spread germs.' She claps her hands and shoos the dog away.

Cases increase in the city. Meetings move online and communal dining areas close. A thermos of green tea and cellophane wrapped sandwiches sits on a trolley in the hotel lobby waiting for guests to collect them. Dr Basu can feel the panic among the delegates. There is talk of ending the conference. A question mark hangs over Dr Basu's paper. He wants to present it in person, use the slides and power point to show how the ancient Egyptians loved and buried their dead.

'No one will bother reading it online. They will skim over it and go back to shopping on Amazon,' he complains to Dr Merton, who whispers about a vendetta against British academics.

Each night, Dr Basu brings his wife up to date with his schedule.

'The sad thing is, Asha, I have yet to present my paper. All this kerfuffle means no one's really interested in my findings.' He had spent years analysing a painted linen mummy shroud dating back to 9 BC and this was the sad outcome. His paper would be a footnote to a flu.

His wife makes soothing noises over the phone. 'Don't worry Dr Basu. Your time to shine will surely come.'

'How is England? Any outbreaks?' He sits as usual on the edge of the bed, in his pyjamas and white sleeveless vest with the pocket sewn in the centre by his wife. This was where he stored his wallet and his passport.

She assures him that things were ticking along just fine at home. A big football match was going ahead in Liverpool, as was the Cheltenham horse race.

'That's good to know,' Dr Basu says. 'But just avoid going out too much. We are not young.'

'You're back soon and...' There is a pause. He hears her cough. When Asha comes back on the phone, her voice lacks its usual bounce.

'You don't sound well, Asha.' Dr Basu pushes the mobile closer to his ear but it doesn't bring his wife any nearer. 'Please take some Lemsip and go back to bed with a hot water bottle. I'll be there soon to look after you.'

'Don't worry. It's just a cold. It's no big deal.' She clears her throat.

Mr Basu isn't convinced. He tries to persuade Dr Merton to join him for dinner at Jaipur Palace.

'It's best not to step out. I'll be dining on cornflakes tonight and green tea.' Dr Merton grimaces and declines.

A thin mist descends from the surrounding hills as Dr

Basu slips out. The streets are ghostly, emptied of sound and movement. A police car passes, its blue light flashing in the dark. It slows down. 'Wear Mask.' The police officer points to his naked mouth.

The restaurant is shut. Dr Basu peers at the orange sign on the rolled down grey shutter but he can't understand the Japanese writing. He returns to the alley where he had first seen the dog. 'Doggy, Doggy.' He whistles into the night. But no dog appears. He heads back to the hotel.

The lobby is swimming in light and noise. Conference delegates crowd around the check-in desks waving bits of paper. Dr Basu spots Dr. Merton.

'What's going on? Is there danger of an earthquake?'

'No, no, much worse.' Dr Merton clasps Dr Basu's hands, his thumbs digging into his soft pink palms.

'Haven't you heard the news? They are cancelling all international flights. We can't get back. We're stuck here ad infinitum.'

'But it can't be.' Dr Basu's mind gallops back to his garden in Woodford, the roses wilting in the evening chill. His wife lay in bed, her body wracked with coughing.

He goes out of the hotel again and searches for a taxi or a bus but none appear. He sees the dog. It lies curled in its usual place, under the lamppost, licking its hind leg.

'Welcome back, dog.' He bends down and rubs its rough, brown back. The dog is weak. It was dying. It was there in the dull glow of his eyes. Dr Basu hadn't spent a life time researching the mourning practices of the old to not

179

recognise when the end was near. The dog begins whimpering.

'Let's go home, friend.' Dr Basu lifts the dog gently, cradling it in his arms as he would a baby and begins running towards the airport.

Acknowledgements

They say it takes a village to raise a child and the same holds true for writing a book. A writer seldom walks alone. Many helping hands have inspired and shaped this collection.

Thank you to all the journals, anthologies and magazines and to BBC Radio 4 for featuring my work.

My heartfelt thanks to Farhana Shaikh for her enthusiasm and belief in my writing. Farhana has consistently championed diverse voices in UK publishing. She is a Superwoman at every level.

Thank you to Dahlia Publishing for their editorial and technical help.

Thank you to The Whole Kahani, writers' collective. Several of these stories were workshopped and analysed over cups of tea on long sunny and cloudy afternoons in London.

Thank you to my parents, Shiv and Krishna Saigal for their encouragement and love. My late father was my biggest fan and his spirit shines over these pages.

Finally, A big Thank you to my husband, Raj and my children Ravi and Sabrina. Your unfailing love and support means the world to me.

About the Author

Reshma Ruia is an award winning writer and poet. Her first novel, *Something Black in the Lentil Soup* was described in the Sunday Times as 'a gem of straight-faced comedy.' Her second novel, *A Mouthful of Silence*, was shortlisted for the SI Leeds Literary Prize. Reshma's short stories and poetry has appeared in British and international journals and anthologies and commissioned for BBC Radio 4. Her debut poetry collection, *A Dinner Party in the Home Counties* won the 2019 Word Masala Award. Reshma has a PhD and Masters in Creative Writing from Manchester University (Distinction) as well as a Bachelor, and a Masters Degree with Distinction from the London School of Economics. She has worked as a development economist with the Food and Agriculture Organisation and the World Food Programme of the UN. She is the co-founder of The Whole Kahani – a writers' collective of British South Asian writers, fiction editor of Jaggery magazine and book reviewer for Words of Colour.

Born in India and brought up in Italy, her writing portrays the inherent preoccupations of those who possess a multiple sense of belonging.

Find out more on her website www.reshmaruia.com or follow her on Twitter @RESHMARUIA.